ALIBI OF GUILT

Cyril Bowers hadn't meant to kill the old man. It was a simple matter of relieving him of a bulging wallet. If the old fool hadn't put up a struggle Cyril wouldn't have hit him.

He wasn't to know that his victim was Dandy Jack Westman's father, but Inspector 'Touchy' Miller knew. He also knew that Dandy Jack would be looking for his father's killer and wouldn't wait for a legal trial for, in Jack's circle, the death penalty had not been abolished.

Jack was working on the details of a wages robbery at the time. The search for the killer and the planning of the robbery seemed to be getting confused.

Confusing to others, perhaps—but not to Dandy Jack.

ALIBI OF GUILT

Philip Daniels

First published in Great Britain 1980
by
Robert Hale Limited
This edition 1996 by Chivers Press
published by arrangement with
the author

ISBN 0 7451 8693 9

British Library Cataloguing in Publication Data available

Printed and bound in Great Britain by
Redwood Books, Trowbridge, Wiltshire

FOREWORD

SOME YEARS BEFORE Jan met him, Dandy Jack's wife had suffered an irreversible mental breakdown, which hardly seems surprising in view of her husband's way of life.

Because of Dandy Jack's willingness to spread around unlimited supplies of cash for information, the police are forced into what appears to be a secondary role, but Inspector Miller comes across as a likable, hardworking character doing his best in difficult circumstances. Inspector Miller illustrates very well the old saying that a policeman's lot is not a happy one. The bane of his life is paperwork, and no matter how hard and long he works at filling in forms he never manages to catch up. On one occasion he spends seventeen consecutive hours on the forms, but at the end of that time he still has some left to complete.

It irritates him when newspapers refer to the rising tide of crime in the metropolis. His solution to that problem would be to cut out all paperwork and send all police officers out on the streets to pursue villains. That, he urges, is what policemen are supposed to do; to catch crooks, not to fill in pieces of paper.

There is a long-standing feud between Inspector Miller and the previously unconvicted Dandy Jack. The Inspector lives in hope that Dandy jack will do something silly that will lead to his arrest; and Dandy Jack, aware of the Inspector's ambition, determines to outwit his old adversary.

The clash of wills between the two men enhances the drama. Which man will win in the end? That question is always uppermost in the reader's mind as the story evolves.

Running alongside the search for the murderer is an investigation into a break-in and wages theft at a factory, and

Inspector Miller has to decide whether the two events are connected. His conclusion leads to a surprising climax.

Peter Chambers has a well-deserved reputation for combining action-filled stories with ingenious and imaginative plots, and this novel is sure to delight his many admirers.

He is adept at leading his readers up the garden path and then astonishing them with a new, but entirely credible, interpretation of events which causes readers to ask themselves: 'Why didn't I think of that?'

If they had thought of it their pleasure in reading the story would have been accordingly diminished, but it is very unlikely that they will be able to compete with the author's ability to puzzle while he entertains.

Peter Chambers is a very prolific writer. His work has been translated into sixteen languages, the latest of which is Indonesian.

In addition to his English thrillers he writes, in the Raymond Chandler tradition, about the engaging private eye Mark Preston, pursuing gangland crime in Monkton City, Southern California.

Whether he is writing about English or American crime, Chambers is always immensely readable and astonishingly versatile.

With sixty titles already in print, he has committed himself to a heavy production schedule, and his readers around the world can be relied on to continue demanding more. He can be relied on not to let them down.

GRANVILLE WILSON

Granville Wilson's publications include crime novels, science fiction books on journalism and short stories. He has also written for radio and television. He worked for many years for British and American newspapers. Born at Castleford, West Yorkshire, he and his wife Irene now live at Hunmanby, North Yorkshire.

ALIBI OF GUILT

ONE

Harry Edwards took a sip of his heavily-watered scotch, and stared hopefully at the clock. Twenty past ten, he registered, and sighed. A lot of people thought being landlord of a public house was the height of ambition. They didn't know how tired a man could get by this time of night. How tired a man's ears could get, with that racket from the so-called musical group in the lounge bar. Drums crashed deafeningly, and there was some thin applause as one of the wailing ditties came to an end.

"Bleedin' row."

A thin-faced man sat hunched at the bar, staring balefully at the landlord.

Harry shrugged.

"It's what they want, nowadays. Anyway, it's not too bad round here. You want to try sitting in the lounge

5

bar. Can't hear yourself drinking round there. 'Orrible."

There was a call from the far end of the bar.

"'Arry. What about some service, then?"

"Coming Mr W."

Old Mr Westman was going it a bit tonight, he reflected. Anniversary of the day he got back to England, after escaping from a prisoner-of-war camp. Well, that was something to celebrate all right. No mistake. Funny, looking at that frail old man, to think of him as he must have been. Young, strong, eager. Cutting his way through barbed wire, and walking through enemy territory all those days. Harry Edwards smiled as he took the empty glass and refilled it with best bitter.

"Pity Jack couldn't get here tonight, Mr W."

Pop Westman grinned.

"He'd have been here if he could, don't you worry. Son and a half, my Jack. Got a bit of business on, that's all. Taking me out tomorrow. Slap-up do, that'll be. Son and a half."

"You're right there."

Harry put money into the till, and went through to check on the lounge bar. The group had started another number, and the flashing blues and yellows from the strobe lighting created a curious visual effect in the crowded room. Harry usually found that ten minutes in the atmosphere was all he could manage without developing a headache. Well, it seemed to suit the young ones all right, he had to admit that. And there were enough of them, packing in like sardines. All drinking nice profitable drinks.

"Everything all right, Elsie?"

"Very good, Mr E. Nice few shillings tonight. Have we got time for a quiet drink afterwards?"

Harry grinned at her fondly. He was very partial to

6

Elsie, the tall, strapping woman who ran this side of the pub with an iron fist. Sometimes, when the missus was away, like tonight, he and Elsie would lock up. Then, depending on how tired they were, they might have a little party of their own.

"I should think so," he replied, "if we can get rid of this lot in a reasonable time. You all right for vodka?"

"Still got two reserves behind the curtain. Should be enough."

He went past her to the till at the far end. Pressing 'No sale' he looked with satisfaction at the packed one and five pound notes. And a few tens, he noted. Well, it would save time later if he started doing a bit of counting now. Especially if Elsie was going to be waiting for him. Reaching inside the machine, he scooped out a handful of notes, and stuffed them in a side pocket.

"Look at that lot, Bas. Just look at it."

A young man at the bar nudged his companion, who was already watching the landlord.

"Must be three or four hundred quid there."

"More than that, Cyril. Not to mention the other bars. I'll bet you he's took a thousand nicker here tonight."

Cyril scowled, and took a swallow at his rum and coke.

"All right for some," he muttered. "And here's me very short on the readies. They'll take that bleeding bike away, you know. What do I do then, eh?"

"You're right there. Got to have a bike. Might as well be dead, otherwise."

"Ere, Bas," Cyril leaned forward confidentially, dropping his tone to a whisper, "you don't suppose we'd have a chance of knocking this bloke over, do you?"

Bas gulped, and stared at him in astonishment.

7

"You'll have to change your drink, old son. Knock him over? A bleeding publican? He's probably got this place locked up like the Bank of England. He's probably got his own private alarm to the pig farm. You have got to be joking, old Cyril. This ain't some back street tobacconist."

Cyril nodded sadly. It was the reaction he'd expected. Indeed it was the reaction he'd have got from any sensible bloke, he had to admit that.

"It's all that money," he said lamely. "And me so short and all."

Bas nodded.

"I know, I know. Tell you what, I've got me eye on a little sweet shop in our own manor. Two old dears run it. Wouldn't be any trouble. Perhaps we'll go and see 'em tomorrow, eh? See how we feel."

"I dunno. I spose so."

Cyril nodded uncertainly. Last one they did fetched exactly eighty four quid. Not exactly the Great Train Robbery. Still, it was cash, and it was easy. If only they spent more time planning things properly, he was sure they could make a decent tickle.

"Oi, I'm thirsty. Is somebody going to do something about it?"

Cyril's sister poked him in the ribs, grinning.

"Oh all right, Sand. My go. What're the others having?"

Bas inspected Sandra as she reeled off a complicated list of drinks. Little darling really, he reflected. Pity about some of that gear she wore, but that wouldn't matter, once he got it off her.

"Good group Bas, innit?"

She turned towards him, a smile playing at the corners of her mouth.

"Bit heavy for me, darling. Like a bit of soul, meself. I know where there's a good place. Take you one night,

8

if you think he'll let you out."

Bas jerked his head towards a tall, fair-haired young man in black leather. Sandra tossed her head.

"Donnie? He's not me bleeding keeper, you know. Don't have to ask him if it's all right to breathe."

"Right then. Come and breathe on me."

She looked at him directly then.

"Tomorrow?"

"Ah well," Bas paused, thinking about his tentative arrangement with Cyril, "might have a bit of business on tomorrow. Day after?"

"If I'm still alive," she shrugged. "We'll see. Me tongue's not hanging out, you know."

"Alf an hour with me darling, and it will be," he promised.

"Fancy yourself, don't you?"

But she was definitely interested, he could tell. They were interrupted by Cyril.

"Is that it, then?"

Sandra counted the glasses on the bar.

"Well," she said in a puzzled tone, "that's what I asked for, but there's only seven drinks there. There's eight of us, you know."

Cyril looked confused, then Bas spoke up.

"You only left me out, that's all. Mean sod. Scotch and American Dry. If you don't mind, that is."

Cyril repeated the order to the waiting Elsie, counting out money onto the bar.

"Won't be enough left for the bus-fare, after this," he grumbled.

Bas chuckled.

"Just see you on a bus," he retorted. "You'd have a job getting that bike up the stairs."

Sandra carried away the last of the drinks to the rest of their party, leaving them alone again.

"'Ave to 'ave a sprinkle," announced Cyril. "You

comin'?"

"No. I'm all right. I'll hang on to your stool."

Cyril walked towards the gents. A hand touched his arm.

"Shouldn't go in there, mate. Bloke 'eaving his lungs up. 'Orrible, it is. There's another one in the saloon. Through that curtain."

Cyril nodded.

"Right, ta."

He threaded his way through the jostling mob, pushed the curtain aside and went through.

In the saloon bar, Pop Westman sat in his favourite chair, close to the door of the gents. The advancing years had accelerated his needs in that direction, and he didn't draw too much attention to his frequent trips if he sat in a handy spot. Two of his cronies were at the table with him, quite willing to listen to his wartime experiences, or anything else he liked to talk about. Always providing of course that he kept a steady supply of beer on the table. Pop didn't mind that. It was the company he enjoyed, and he was quite willing to pay out more than his fair share. After all, these other men weren't so lucky. Didn't have a son like his Jack. Not many people did, and that was a fact.

"Evening, gents. Anything for the Boys Club tonight?"

A man stood by the table, smiling down at Pop and his friends. In his hands was a wooden box, with a wide slit in the top, and the legend 'St Mark's Boys' Club' hand-painted on the side.

"Blimey, is it Tuesday already?" sighed one of the old men, rooting in his pocket.

"Now, now," reproved Pop. "Many's the night you and me were glad of the club in the old days. Nice game of billiards, and nothing to pay. We always knew where to get a free cup of tea."

Reaching inside his jacket he pulled out his wallet. One of the high spots of his week, Tuesday night. While everyone else was fiddling with small change, ten pence here, twenty there, yes, and five if they thought nobody was looking, he always made the grand gesture. Jack always impressed it on him.

"Now don't forget, Dad. This is all for you. Do what you like with it. Go chasing the birds up the other end if you want to. Your money, this is. But this fiver here, this is separate. This is for the Club. Tuesday night, now, don't forget. That lot, yours. This five, the Boys' Club."

As though he was likely to forget, after all the Club had meant to him as a boy. And to Jack, later. Especially Jack. That's where he really learned his boxing, down at the Club.

He opened the wallet carefully, letting the others see the packed banknotes. Drawing out a five pound note with a great flourish, he made a display of inserting it in the top of the box.

"That's from both of us," he announced. "Me, and my son Jack. I expect you remember him, all right?"

The collector smiled.

"Everybody round here remembers Dandy Jack," he acknowledged. "And thank you very much, Mr Westman. Very generous of you. Both of you."

One of the others leaned over the table, dropping in coins. At the same time, he muttered.

"Don't you think you ought to put that wallet away? Shouldn't oughta be flashing that sort of money around. Never know who's watching."

"We're all friends here," grumbled Pop. "Besides, nobody's going to mess about with me. People know who I am."

"Ted's right, though" contributed another of his friends. "Asking for trouble, really."

11

A young man walked past towards the gents, pushed at the door and went inside. As the door closed behind him, Cyril's mind was racing. There must have been well over fifty quid in that old geezer's leather. Could have been as much as a hundred. Think of it. Silly old sod like that, with all that money. That was wrong, that was. All wrong. He leaned against a dirty washbasin, thinking. If this had been his own local, he would have known the old man, by sight at least. That would have helped him to know what to do. But this was strange territory. The old feller could be anybody. Might even live on the premises, for all he knew. Cyril felt at a disadvantage.

Another man came in, and walked over to the urinals. Cyril ran the cold tap, making a show of splashing water on his face. When the stranger was finished, he paused before leaving.

"You all right?" he queried.

Cyril nodded. Nosy bastard.

"Yeah. Bit funny, that's all. Too hot round there."

"I'll bet it is. Bleedin' row."

The other man went away. Cyril felt around for a handkerchief to dry his face. This would be one in the eye for Bas, he reflected. Never mind about him and his sweetshop. This was ready money, and for the taking. All they had to do was wait outside. If the old man came out mob-handed, then they could do a fast melt. But if he came out by himself, it was a simple case of following him. Once they got clear of the pub, if him and Bas couldn't sort out one old man it would be a fine lookout. And then, a whole new thought occurred to Cyril. Why did he need Bas at all? It was only one old man. Probably half-pissed at that. Dark outside. Why split with Bas? He could keep all the money for himself. The thought was a complete novelty. Him and Bas did everything together. Always had. He'd never attempted anything like this by himself. It was his case, though. He found the old man in the first place, didn't he? Why should he have to share? He could pay off for that sodding bike, and still have a few readies left over. Nothing to do with Bas, really. No need for him to know. Have to shake him off, though. Think of a yarn.

Cyril squared his shoulders, conscious of having made a decision of some importance. He was about to strike out on his own, for the first time. That was a big step, that.

Harry Edwards was lighting a cigar as Cyril stepped out into the bar. What was he doing round this side, he wondered? He didn't want the lounge crowd spilling over into the saloon. The saloon was for his regulars, the local people. Ah, he was going back where the noise was. That was all right then.

Cyril went back to the waiting Bas, noting that his sister had returned to where Donnie was watching the band.

"Took you long enough," greeted Bas. "You been having a crafty one round there, on your own?"

Cyril kept his voice low.

"Had a bit of luck Bas. There's a little darling round there. I've seen her before, and she was definitely showing for me."

Bas was sceptical.

"In the balloon?" he queried. "What's she doing in the balloon, then? In a wheelchair, or something?"

"Not yet. She hasn't upset me yet," grinned Cyril. "No, it's some kind of family do. Lot of old people, you know. Thought I'd give her a chance. Be turning out time soon."

The news did not please his friend.

"What about me, then? Has she got a friend, or what?"

"Not this time, old son. Look, I'll be as quick as I

can. Might be back before you pack up. If not, see you tomorrow."

Bas shrugged.

"Well, if you're that desperate. Can't have you coming out in spots. I'm not hanging about, though."

"Right. Don't say nothing to Sand. Tell her I had a gutsache."

Cyril made his way carefully around the edge of the packed bar, watching Sandra and the others, to be certain they didn't notice his departure. Then he was outside. The night was chilly and dark, but at least the rain had stopped. The first job was to shift that motor bike over to a far corner, where the others wouldn't spot it when they left.

Tom Crabtree closed the door of the saloon bar, and stepped out into the night, buttoning up his coat. Seemed a bit colder this year, somehow. People tried to tell you it wasn't the weather at all, it was you getting older, but Tom would have none of that. He wasn't old at all, not really. Not in these days, when people lived to be a hundred. There was a bloke in Russia, it was in the papers, this bloke was a hundred and thirty two. Now, that was old, you'd have to admit that. Besides, he'd stayed till closing time, same as always. It was when you started going home early, that was when you were old. Like old Westman tonight. You could probably put that down to old age.

Tom crossed the road, turning the corner at the little grocer's shop, and into the street where he had lived for the past forty years. Definitely colder tonight. Dark too. As he passed the alleyway, which people used as a short cut through to the market, the low cloud shifted suddenly, and pale moonlight filtered through. Hallo. What was that? Looked as though somebody had dumped a heap of rubbish in the entrance there. He

14

drew closer, and caught his breath. What he was looking at was the figure of a man, crumpled up. Must be ill, or something. Fearfully, and looking all around, he knelt down beside the prostrate body.

Blimey, it was old Westman. Heart attack, that's what it was. No, wait a minute, was that blood on his head? It was blood. Gawd's truth.

Thoroughly frightened now, Tom got to his feet, and turned back towards the pub. This was too much for him. He needed somebody in authority, and his mind turned at once to the licensee, Harry Edwards. Yes, yes, that was it.

Harry would know what to do.

TWO

Jan Stewart looked at her watch for the hundredth time. Only eleven thirty. That meant Jack wouldn't be home for another three hours at least, probably four. There wasn't any guarantee as to time when he was on one of his card parties. Crossing to the window, she pushed the button to draw back the electrically-operated curtains, and stared down into the Kensington night. There was plenty going on down there, as she had reason to know, and until she became involved with Dandy Jack Westman, Jan had been very much a part of the scene. These days, when he wasn't with her, she sat around at home, taking endless baths and setting her hair. She took a cigarette from a mahogany box, and lit it from the heavy ivory table-lighter, smiling at her own thoughts. Jan Stewart, the little woman at home. It was ridiculous, and there were still a lot of people around who wouldn't believe it. Or didn't want to.

"Come on, Jan. It's not as though you're doing anything else. Jack's out that evening, you said so yourself."

How to explain? How do you tell people, who've known you for years as a hell-raiser, that it's different now? Jan hadn't spent an evening at home since the dark ages. Never had a home, not in any real sense. Always some pokey flat or other, strewn with discarded bits of underwear, and a sink piled high with half-scraped plates. There was never any time for cleaning or tidying up. Always some new, vitally important commitment to be met. Until Jack. The world changed then. Imperceptibly at first, but steadying down with increasing seriousness, as the early weeks went by. Finally, this.

She looked around at the tastefully furnished living room. A real home, at last. Tidy, to boot. Jack was essentially a tidy person, and although he was not the type to nag, Jan had simply found herself wanting to keep the place the way he liked it..Wanting to please the man. That was a departure in itself. And not one she could explain, except deep within herself. Certainly, it would never have been possible to any of the old crowd.

"Westman, Westman? Can't recall any Westman."

"Some kind of gambler, they say."

"Pots of the stuff, has he? I mean, he'd need pots to keep up with Jan, wouldn't he?"

"Tim says he's a gangster."

"Probably going to sell her off to one of those Arab johnnies, I shouldn't wonder. She'll wind up in Saudi or somewhere, in chains."

"Ella said she saw them at the White Slipper the other night. You know what an arrogant bastard Louis is, the head waiter? Well, according to Ella, he was fawning all over this Westman."

17

"There you are, then. He only fawns over Arabs and gangsters. Only way I can account for her behaviour."

Jan smiled at her own thoughts, and walked across to press a cassette into the machine. One thing about being by herself, one small advantage, was that she could listen to some of her beloved jazz without Jack making a protesting exit to the bedroom. That was one of the many little incongruities about the man. Everything about him told you he would be a jazz enthusiast. And everything told you wrong. His scene was the music of Old Vienna, the sugared violins etc. Well, he wasn't here at the moment, and so she could have the MJQ up at full blast.

It was at the end of the first track that she realised the telephone was ringing. Dismissing a momentary impulse to ignore it, she reached over and picked up the slim leather-covered handpiece.

"Hallo?"

"Mr Westman, please."

A man's voice, deepish and slightly Cockney.

"I'm sorry, he's not here at the moment. Can I take a message?"

At the other end, Harry Edwards frowned. This would be the posh bird Jack was shacked up with.

"It's very important," he told her. "Have you got a number where I could reach him, please?"

"No, I'm sorry," Jan resisted. "Can't it wait until tomorrow?"

"Definitely not," was the reply. "Look, if you can't give me another number, is there some way you might be able to get a message to him? This is urgent, top priority, believe me."

Jan hesitated. It was clear from the caller's tone that it was urgent, so far as he was concerned. Whether Jack would consider it urgent enough to justify calling him away from his game was another matter entirely.

18

"That would be very difficult," she hedged. "Perhaps if you could tell me something about it?"

Stupid cow, fumed Harry. It was trouble enough having to be the one to give Dandy Jack the bad news. The alternative, to be the one who failed to get the message delivered, would put him in a position he didn't care to dwell on. Swallowing his rising impatience, he said.

"Look miss, I appreciate your position, but this is very important indeed. Believe me, I'm not the man to bother Dandy Jack if I thought I'd be wasting his time."

Jan nibbled at her lower lip, considering.

"Who is this?"

"My name is Edwards, Harry Edwards. I'm the landlord of the Hope and Anchor, Jack's old pub. It's about his father, miss. There's some bad news, and I must get through."

His father? That sweet old man Jack doted on. Jan had met him a couple of times, and knew well the strong bond between them. If the old boy was ill, that was certainly something Jack would want to know, and at once. In point of fact, she didn't know exactly where he was, but in a case of emergency she always had to contact one of his two inseparable companions, his stooges as she considered them privately.

"Very well, I'll see if I can get in touch with him. Can I ring you back in about five minutes?"

Five minutes. Harry considered this. It meant more delay in contacting the law, and they wouldn't like that. He'd have to play stupid. Have to tell them there was nothing to report unless a doctor had definitely declared the old man to be dead. There was a doctor on the way already, and once he'd pronounced his verdict there was no way Harry could justify not calling in the police. Problem was, he couldn't tell all that to this bird. She might go off in a dead faint or something equally useless.

He took a deep breath.

"Five minutes is a long time, miss. Couldn't you try to do it in two? Jack won't thank me for any delay."

The man was clearly worried about Jack's reaction. Jan was intrigued. It was her first experience of what effect the name of Jack Westman could have, out in that other world of his, which he kept away from her.

"I'll be as quick as I can, Mr Edwards. What's your number, please?"

In a room challenging the clouds above Hyde Park, five men sat around a table, four of them watching closely the hands of the fifth man as he dealt new cards from a silver-backed pack. They had been playing for an hour, and it was too early to predict how the evening would turn out. There was a two a.m. limit, because two men had a plane to catch, but two a.m. was a long way off yet.

The best-dressed man of the group was Dandy Jack Westman, who hadn't been given his nickname without cause. As the last card landed before him, he scooped up all five, dragging them over the green baize and up close to his face.

King, Two, King, Ace, Seven.

Good start. It was beginning to look as though tonight was going to be good all round. He was already over two hundred and fifty pounds ahead of the game, although no one knew better than he how quickly that could change.

"Ten."

The first player pushed a brown chip into the middle. It was a something and nothing opener. The first two rounds never meant anything. Jack picked up one of his own chips, waiting for his turn. In a corner of the room, a pink telephone shrilled. The dealer shrugged, and stood up, walking over to the instrument.

"It's for you, Jack."

The others frowned, but said nothing.

Jack Westman placed his cards face down on the table, and went over to the phone.

"Who is this?" he said carefully.

After that, he listened. His face gave little away, but the others noted the way his body straightened gradually.

"You done the right thing, Harry," he pronounced finally. "Now hear this. The word down there is stumm. You understand me, Harry? I'm relying on you to make sure everybody understands what I say. Stumm. No, I don't know when I'll get there. You'll have to wait up."

Without waiting for confirmation of his instructions, he replaced the receiver with great care. Then he turned around to the others.

"Sorry about this. I'm going to have to pack it in."

The others exchanged glances. It was a very serious matter to walk out on a game at this level. They didn't like it.

"Something important Jack, is it?"

One man spoke for them all.

Jack nodded. He knew only too well what it meant to upset people of their standing.

"It's the old man. My father. Somebody just killed him."

Some of the tension went from the atmosphere. The man who had asked the question pursed his lips.

"Well, that certainly makes a difference, as far as I'm concerned. Sorry to hear your bad news."

"Yeah. Sorry to hear that, Jack."

Another man spoke up. The other two said nothing.

"I take nothing out. There's over two hundred and fifty there. You can put it in the middle, or divvy it up.

Whatever you want. But I've got to go."

He turned away, and walked out of the room.

No one said 'good night'.

Inspector Ronald Joseph Miller yawned, and looked at his wristwatch. Midnight. He'd been on duty since seven in the morning, so that made, let's see, seventeen hours. Seventeen bloody hours of consecutive duty, and still he hadn't caught up with his paperwork. Thirty minutes, he decided. Thirty minutes more, and that was going to be it. A copper could work twenty four hours a day, every day, and still be behind. It always made him irritable when people carried on about recruitment difficulties, the rising tide of crime in the metropolis, and all the other newspaper labels which were trotted out at regular intervals. Mostly, he noted, when there was a shortage of hard overseas news, or a brief respite from industrial problems. The solution was quite clear to Inspector Miller. You simply cut out all paperwork, and instructed all police officers to get out on the street, and pursue villains. That was what coppers were supposed to do, wasn't it? Catch crooks? Not fill in pieces of paper.

He stared unlovingly at the neat pile of green and pink forms which lay before him on the desk. Thirty minutes only, he promised himself.

"Sorry to interrupt, inspector."

Miller looked up at the sound of the station sergeant's voice.

"What is it, Rookie?"

"Possible murder case. Outside the Hope and Anchor, in Deacon Street. P.C. Cooper's been on, calling for C.I.D."

The inspector drew in his breath sharply, sleep dropping away from his mind on the instant.

"Cooper, eh? Level-headed bloke, that. What do you

22

think?"

Sergeant Rook nodded seriously.

"Sounds as if he might be right. An elderly man is the victim, badly damaged about the head. He was found in the street just round the corner from the pub. Cooper is satisfied he didn't get the injuries simply from falling over. Or being hit by a car."

"H'm."

Murder, eh? It had been over a year since there'd been a murder on the patch. Just his luck to miss it, since he wasn't the duty officer. He repeated the thought aloud.

"Just my luck, eh Rookie? Lofty is on his way, I suppose?"

The sergeant shook his head.

"That's just it. Inspector Fennimore is already out, following up that tip on a break-in, down at the blanket factory. I thought you'd be especially interested. The dead man is Pop Westman. Dandy Jack's father."

Miller whistled softly, rising to his feet.

"Blimey," he muttered. "The fur will fly now. To think I nearly went home a quarter of an hour ago. I wouldn't even have known."

Rook nodded. He and Inspector Miller were old friends, and he was well aware of the long-standing feud between the policeman and the hitherto unconvicted Dandy Jack. He watched the grin which developed slowly at the corners of the inspector's mouth.

"Dandy Jack's old man, eh? This will upset Mr Westman Junior, I fancy. A few other heads will get bashed before we get this one sorted out. We'd better find the culprit, quick. If Westman catches him first, he'll never see a courtroom, that's a racing certainty."

"When a man's upset, he does silly things sometimes. Perhaps Jack will do something silly, and we can have him."

Miller looked grave.

"Exactly what I'm thinking. I'm glad I didn't go home. Better get down there right away. Do me a favour, Rookie. Get the feelers out. Find out where the O'Connell brothers are tonight."

Dessie and Dave O'Connell were a pair of villains responsible for a fair proportion of police activity in the manor. They were also old adversaries of Dandy Jack Westman's. Even so, killing a harmless old man, simply because he was Jack's father, seemed unlikely to Sergeant Rook.

"You don't suppose they did this, surely?"

"I'm not supposing anything," retorted Miller. "Just like to know what they're up to, that's all. It's something Jack will be wanting to know, as well. We might as well know it first. I just hope he hasn't had a chance to drop a blanket over this lot yet."

The sergeant knew what he meant. If the locals were warned not to cooperate with the police, then the investigation could get very seriously clogged.

"I doubt it," he replied. "Cooper was only a couple of streets away when the call came in. He was on the scene in less than five minutes."

Miller put his papers into a tidy pile.

"Right. I'm off. Better get on to Lofty, and tell him I'm just putting in an appearance till he's able to get there."

Rook nodded impassively. He knew perfectly well that Touchy Miller had no intention of letting Fennimore, or anybody else, get near any investigation which promised a chance of nobbling Dandy Jack Westman.

Out loud, he said.

"Just holding the fort, like."

"That's it."

The inspector winked as he went out.

24

THREE

In life, Pop Westman had not been a tall man, but he had always walked with his back straight, head held high, and no one thought of him as in any way small. Now, the dignity of life stripped away, he was a pathetic shrunken copy of his former self, as he lay on a hastily improvised bed in the saloon bar of the Hope and Anchor. A sheet had been drawn over him, and pulled up to cover the awful damage done to his head and face.

There was no talking among the six people in the bar, each of them busy with private thoughts. Behind the counter, Harry Edwards rested his elbows, watching the door and waiting for the dead man's son to appear. He'd done all he could, he was quite satisfied about that, but if Jack didn't get here soon, the C.I.D. people would be in. The questions would start then, and no mistake. Although the landlord had warned people to

25

keep their mouths shut, using Dandy Jack's name in the process, he was by no means certain it was going to work. Not once those plain-clothes men started in with their deadly, seemingly harmless questions. What was needed, to reinforce the warning, was the presence of the man himself.

Beside him, Elsie went about the routine business of tidying up after the evening session, gathering glasses, rinsing them in the boiling, soapy water, and drying them off. It was good to have Elsie there, with her calm, reassuring efficiency. She had intended to remain behind tonight in any case, Harry remembered, but not to help him tidy up. There had been quite a different ending planned for the evening. Ah, well.

Seated in huddled silence around a table by the door were the only three remaining customers. Tom Crabtree was there, turning his pint mug endlessly on the plastic surface. Tom's thoughts were in something of a turmoil. His had been the gloomy distinction of discovering the body, and that would bring him a little glory for the next few days. Be good for quite a few pints, that would, what with the newspapers and all. That was one side of it. The other was the less attractive prospect of trying to keep things from the police. It was all very fine for the landlord to pass on his little message for Dandy Jack. He wasn't the one who would have to dodge the questions. How could a man dodge questions, anyway? What was he supposed to say?

"Sorry officer, I made a mistake. I didn't find the body at all. Matter of fact, I'm not even here. Must be a case of mistaken identity."

Was that what Jack expected? No. It couldn't be that. What, then? Because there was no mistaking Harry Edwards' words. Dandy Jack certainly expected something. From all of them, not just him. But him, in particular, of course. Because he found him, found old

Pop. Funny, really. He'd been in two minds about whether to stop at home tonight, and watch the football. Funny how things turn out. You never know.

His companions at the table stared around the bar from time to time. They weren't quite certain what they were doing here. They didn't know anything about any murder. It was only a matter of pure chance that they were still in the bar when Tom came rushing in with his ghastly news. Not fair, really.

The last person present was P.C. Cooper. A young, but well-experienced officer, he was in on the ground floor with his first case of murder, and finding his role unrewarding. Having taken the names of those present, there was nothing for him to do but ensure they remained on the premises, and also keep an eye on the body. Questions were a matter for C.I.D., and all he could do was stand around. A policeman's lot, and all that.

The brass-bound door of the bar opened suddenly inwards, and three men advanced inside. P.C. Cooper straightened at once. He didn't know the faces, but he knew the style. The first man was about six feet tall, with broad muscular shoulders beneath an expensive dark-blue suit. Thick black curly hair surmounted a face on which the smile-lines were clearly etched, despite the present grim set of the features. This man ignored the policeman, ignored everyone, and walked quickly over to the tell-tale sheet.

A powerful hand gripped at one corner, pulling it gently aside. There was silence in the bar, even more profound than before.

The new arrival made a choking sound, and large tears formed in his eyes, coursing unheeded down his face as he stared at the ruined head.

The other two newcomers had remained just inside the door. One of them nodded imperceptibly at Harry

Edwards, who nodded back. Well, he reflected, Jack was here now. They were all here now, and it was out of his hands. The man who had nodded was Georgie Parks, the number two man on Jack's team. The third one was Big Bill Yateley, so-called because he was only five feet four inches tall, but a terrible man in an upset. The publican felt relieved. He'd done all he could, and now the principals could take over.

"Mr Jack Westman, is it?"

Dandy Jack turned towards the questioner, bobbed his head, and looked back at his dead father for the last time. Then he replaced the sheet, smoothing gently.

"That's me, officer," he confirmed.

"Very sorry about this terrible business, Mr Westman. The C.I.D. officers will be here at any moment. There isn't much I can do until they arrive. Er, these other gentlemen, Mr Westman?"

"Friends of the family," replied Jack tersely. "Close friends of the family."

He took a large, snowy handkerchief from his pocket, dabbing at his face. Then he blew his nose violently, drawing in several deep breaths. It was over now. The worst time had been when he first heard on the telephone. That, and the awful ride in the car coming down here. Trying to convince himself that it wasn't true. Trying to convince himself that it was true. There must have been some mistake. There hadn't been any mistake. Harry Edwards was a level-headed man, a straight man. He wouldn't get a thing like this wrong. And, of course, he hadn't. The old man was dead. Murdered. There were no two ways of looking at that. Somebody, some bastard, had killed his father. That was all there was to it. Now that the fact was established, there were things to be done. Well, only one thing really, when you boiled it down.

He, Jack Westman, would find the murdering

bastard, and kill him.

Everybody would have to help him. Not the police, naturally. They didn't understand about things like this, and they'd probably even get in his way. But everybody else would help, because Christ help them if they didn't.

"Harry," he turned towards the bar, "you've got my private bottle of brandy that I bought the the other week. Let's have a drop. One for everybody, it's a cold night."

Edwards nodded, reaching behind him. There wasn't any private bottle belonging to Jack, but it was a way of circumventing the licensing law. The policeman probably wouldn't have made any fuss, in the circumstances, but Jack wasn't going to take the chance. Harry wasn't remotely concerned about the money for the drink. Jack Westman was a man who paid his debts. As the thought entered his head, the publican looked across at the white-sheeted tables. He shuddered. Oh, yes, there was no doubt about that.

Jack Westman always paid his debts.

"You're more than welcome, officer," advised Jack, "but I expect you'll leave it out, eh? Being on duty."

P.C. Cooper nodded. He wasn't in the slightest deceived by the talk of Westman's private purchase, but this was no time to be standing on his dignity. He remembered his old sergeant's words.

"There's the law, son, and then there's the law. If you're chasing a couple of armed villains, you don't stop to book somebody else for parking on a yellow line."

"No thank you, Mr Westman. But no disrespect, you understand."

Jack nodded, picking up the glass set ready for him, and signalling across to his companions. Big Bill Yateley collected three of the drinks, and carried them over to where the three elderly men were sitting. Tom

Crabtree raised his glass towards the dead man, and his companions followed suit. No one spoke. Then there came the sound of voices from the lounge bar.

Westman shot an enquiring glance at the landlord.

"That's the band, Jack," explained Harry. "Takes 'em a time to pack up their clobber. They were still here when—when it happened. So the officer said they'd have to stay till the C.I.D. came."

"Band, eh? Busy night next door, was it?"

"Busy enough," Harry confirmed. "Must have been close to a hundred and fifty of 'em in there."

A hundred and fifty. That was bad. That could make things very complicated, reflected Jack. Locals were one thing, but these young ones were a different proposition altogether. They came from all over, if there was a group they wanted to hear. Sod it. This could make life difficult.

"Billy."

Yateley came to his side.

"Do me a favour, Billy. Take one round for the band, will you? How many of 'em, Harry?"

"Four."

"Right, four it is. And Billy," Jack lowered his voice to little more than a whisper, "make sure they understand how things are. Find out where I can get in touch with 'em. You know."

The short man nodded, collecting the tin tray on which Harry had set the four glasses, and making his way through into the lounge bar.

As he disappeared, the street door opened again, and two men walked in. P.C. Cooper straightened himself up. It was out of his hands now.

"Well Jack, I'm sorry to hear all this bad news."

"Hallo, inspector."

It would have to be Touchy Miller, of course. Bit of bad luck, that. Miller had been dying to pin something on him for years. Not that he'd let that influence the investigation. Good copper, Miller. But Jack would have to be extra careful while this particular policeman was around.

The inspector was staring impassively down at the dead man.

"Bad business," he muttered. "Now then everybody, I know you all want to give us every assistance. I also know it's late at night, and you'll want to be getting off as soon as you can. I won't keep you any longer than is absolutely necessary. To start with, will you please give your names and addresses to the sergeant here. Give me a minute, constable."

Cooper and the inspector walked to a far corner of the bar, conversing quietly. Jack leaned on the bar, and Harry Edwards craned forward to hear what he said.

"Appreciate what you did, Harry. You managed to tell people what I said, did you?"

"Deaf, dumb and blind, all of 'em," was the reply. "People round here think—thought—a lot of your father, Jack. Should be all right."

"Well, we'll have a bit of a chat, after we get rid of the filth."

The quiet exchange did not escape Inspector Miller, and he would dearly have loved to be a box of matches on the counter. Dismissing the constable, he walked back to the bar, staring pointedly at the landlord. Harry moved away, leaving the policeman alone with the son of the dead man.

"This is bad business, Jack."

"Right."

"We're not the best of mates, you and me, but don't make any mistakes. Your father was well respected. I'll find out who did this, and I'll have him."

"Hope you do. And I wish you luck."

The two men stared at each other.

"Just one more thing, Jack. There's only one law here, and I'm it. I know how you must feel—"

"—do you?—"

"—and I can't have you going around knocking on doors. This is a matter for the police. Leave us to get on with it. Otherwise—"

He left the sentence uncompleted, and shrugged.

"You were saying?"

Jack's eyes were unwavering.

"You know what I'm saying. If you start meddling, interfering with witnesses, stuff like that, I'll have you."

There was no expression on the other man's face when he replied.

"Why inspector, I'm surprised at you. As though I'd do such a thing. Don't fancy myself as Dick Barton. That's your job, that is. That's why I pay all these taxes, innit?"

The inspector was unmoved by the announcement.

"Started paying taxes, have you? The Chancellor of the Exchequer must have been surprised. Anyway, remember what I said. Hands off."

Jack turned away then.

"Where's that bottle, Harry?"

It was going to be a long night.

At about the time Jack Westman and his men arrived at the Hope and Anchor, another man walked in at a narrow doorway in a Soho side street. Closing a shabby door behind him, he stepped into a carpeted hallway. At the far end, a man in a blue dinner jacket sat behind a small, desk, watching his approach.

"Good evening, sir. Are you a member?"

The newcomer was taken aback at this unexpected greeting. He'd give him 'member', cheeky sod, but words died in his throat as a second man appeared

32

suddenly from behind a mauve velvet curtain,

"Well, well," grinned the second man, "look who's here. You didn't answer the gentleman, Maxie. Are you a proper member of this licensed rat-hole?"

Maxie swallowed, then achieved a nervous smile.

"Oh hallo, Mr Small. Long time no see. Yes, I'm a member. All paid up and everything. Very legitimate place, this is. Very straight. Didn't know you belonged, though."

Mr Small nodded.

"I belong everywhere, Maxie. Everywhere there's vermin. Like you, and your friends inside. Pest control officer, that's me. Watch out, next time you see me. Might be your turn to get sprayed."

He walked past the now silent Maxie, who watched him carefully until the street door closed behind him.

"I'll 'ave 'im, one of these days," he breathed. "One of these fine days, I'll spread him all over a wall."

The man at the desk said nothing. Max Bloom was a man of unpredictable temperament, violence simmering constantly just below the surface, and he'd just been compelled to swallow an insult. Whatever anybody said could be the wrong thing, for the next few minutes.

Bloom breathed heavily, as he struggled to calm himself. His temper would be the undoing of him one day, and he knew it. With a mighty effort, he pulled himself together.

"Des inside?" he asked.

"They both are," was the reply.

Max nodded, dragging the heavy curtain aside, and stepping into the darkened room beyond. At a corner table sat the group he was looking for. Two large cheerful-faced men, with their arms around two girls who could have stepped straight out of a television commercial. One of the men spotted him, and a booming voice sounded across the smoke-laden room.

33

"Maxie boy. Over 'ere."

The girls looked up with interest at the new arrival.

"Siddown, Maxie. 'Ave a drink. We'll have to see if we can't find something else for you to have, in a minute. These two are taken."

Desmond O'Connell winked at him.

"Allo Des. Davie."

The other man smiled cheerfully, and winked.

"Girls, this is Maxie. Mate of ours, so you be nice. Not too nice, mind. It's our booze."

The girls flashed their brilliant teeth at him, and Max pulled over a padded chair to join them. They made a good-looking picture, the girls and the handsome O'Connell brothers.

"You just missed another old mate," confided Des. "Pincher Small's been in."

"I seen him outside," replied Max. "What's he sniffing about for, did he say?"

"No," scoffed Dave. "Just come in to get a warm, I expect. Never even spoke to us. I was offended, I was. Did he say anything to you?"

"Just the usual," shrugged Max. "I felt like smearing him."

"Tut tut," reproved Des. "What a terrible thing to say. Anyway, don't let him spoil the party. Thought you wasn't coming in till later, Max."

It was a question. Max looked uncertainly at the girls.

"I wasn't really, but I had a bit of news. Thought you ought to know about it."

Dave cleared his throat.

"This is the news at midnight," he proclaimed solemnly, "presented by Max Bloom. Go on then, son."

Max hesitated.

"I wouldn't want to bore the girls."

"Ah."

Des withdrew his arm from the nearest girl's waist at

34

once.

"Get lost," he said tersely.

"Des" squealed his partner.

"You heard him," said Dave. Then, turning to his own partner, he added "You too. Go and powder your fanny, or something."

"Charming, I'm sure."

The girls stood up, retrieved their little handbags, treated all three of them to a snort of annoyance, and swept away.

"What's up, Maxie?"

By common consent, the three men had all dropped their heads forward, into a small confidential triangle.

"It's old Pop Westman, Dandy Jack's father, I spect you know him."

The brothers exchanged glances.

"We know him. What about him?"

"Somebody scragged him tonight."

"What?"

Dave let out a small whistle.

"Who done him?" he demanded.

"I don't know no more than I've said."

Des frowned.

"Who told you?"

"Jack had a game tonight. Hadn't got properly started when he had this phone call. He just walked out."

"Did he, be gawd."

This was news indeed. For a professional gambler of Dandy Jack's class to walk out of a game was unthinkable. It was all the confirmation the O'Connells needed that Max's information had to be correct.

"Who'd want to hurt a nice old man like that?" wondered Des. "I had a drink with him meself the other week. What was he, shot or what?"

"I don't know," returned Max. "I only know it

happened."

"There'll be trouble," muttered Dave.

Des nodded his agreement.

"That there will. Wonder if that's why the Pincher stuck his head in here just now. You know, just having a little sniff round, seeing where every body is."

"Could be," agreed Dave. "Well, Max my son, this is not the best news I ever heard. Jack's going to be a very cross man till this gets sorted out. Des, we ought to be having a serious talk. How would you feel if we dumped these two scrubbers?"

Des made a face of resignation.

"Plenty more where they came from. We'll lose 'em. Let's get a few bottles in, and go back to the flat."

They all stood up, and one or two faces turned as they made their way towards the door. If anyone wondered where they were going, no one voiced the question.

When the O'Connell brothers and Maxie Bloom were on the roam, it was a good time to mind your own business.

FOUR

Jack Westman closed the door of the flat as quietly as he could. It was three thirty in the morning, and he was trying to avoid waking Jan. He pushed home the burglar-lock with great care. These expensive blocks of flats were a gift to the light-fingered trade. It wouldn't do for a well-known figure like himself to be done over.

It was doubtful whether he'd be able to sleep, he admitted. There was too much going on inside his head. What was the word? Turmoil. That was it. Too much turmoil. Crossing to the kitchen, he switched on a small lamp, which was all he'd need for making a cup of coffee. The place was immaculate as always, and he noted this with satisfaction. Full of surprises, that was Jan. When they'd agreed to set up house, Jack had expected a steady diet of frozen food and a mountain of unwashed plates. You couldn't really expect much else from a posh bird like Jan Stewart. Probably never had to do a hand's turn in her life. But he had been wrong about her. She was an excellent cook, with a sharp eye for the fresher vegetables and any bargains at the butchers. Jack had never eaten so well in his life. Amazing girl, she was.

As the kettle boiled, he sensed rather than heard her enter the kitchen.

"Tried not to wake you, love."

"I know, but I was half-listening for you. Let me do that."

He stood aside, letting her take charge, then sat down at the breakfast bar, and waited. Jan came over with two steaming mugs, setting one before him. Reaching over, she pressed his hand.

"If you feel like telling me, I'm here."

Jack had always made it clear that questions were unwelcome, and in a sense she was cut off from a part of his life, the outside man whom she scarcely knew. But tonight was different. There was an odd set to his face, almost as though a skin-tight mask had been drawn over it, in order to prevent any emotion from registering. In a way that was what had happened. For this was the gambler's mask, the face he presented when so much depended on chance, as well as skill. It was curiously appropriate, too, though Jan had no way of knowing it. Because in the past few hours Dandy Jack Westman had committed himself to the greatest gamble he would ever undertake, and the stake was his own life.

Now, as he sat looking at the concern on the girl's face, he wanted desperately to confide in her, to pour out the misery and the hate, to share the awful isolation he felt. It would be so easy, and he knew the comfort it would bring to his troubled mind. In the same instant, he dismissed the thought. The path he had chosen was narrow and dangerous, with pitfalls at every turn.

38

There was no room on it for two.

"Of course I'm going to tell you," he assured her. "It's my father. When he left the pub tonight, somebody hit him, to steal his money. Whoever it was, they hit him too hard. He's dead, Jan."

As he spoke the last words, his eyes brimmed over with tears. Funny, that. He would have sworn he had himself under control. Jan moved swiftly round the table and stood beside him, cradling his head against her. He felt himself relax against her warm comfort. She stared down at the thick curly hair, compassion deep and strong within her. A hundred questions jostled for prominence inside her head, but she thrust them resolutely aside.

"We'll talk about it tomorrow," she told him softly. "There'll be plenty to do then. Come to bed. Come on, now."

She raised him gently up, and led him out.

Inspector Miller hung up his coat, lifted out his notebook and went wearily over to his desk. A young constable came into the room, set down a steaming mug and went quickly away. One look at the inspector's face told him that absence was the best policy. They didn't call the guvnor 'Touchy' for nothing.

The seated man picked up the hot drink and sipped at it. He'd often discussed with fellow-officers whether the people who made police-station tea were committing a crime or only a misdemeanour. Ah well. At least it was hot.

There was a tap at the door, and Sergeant Rook put his head into the room.

"Come in, Rookie."

The tone of his voice told the sergeant that the inspector's enquiries had not been very productive.

"How did it go?" he ventured.

Miller snorted.

"Go? It didn't go at all. It was like trying to start a motor car with no bleeding engine, that's how it went. What is it they always say in those prisoner-of-war films? Name, rank and serial number. That's it." He tapped at the book in front of him. "That's what I've got in there. Names, ranks, and serial sodding numbers. Nothing else. Do you know, some of those lovely witnesses had a job remembering what it was they'd been drinking. You'd have thought I was asking them for the plans of the Allied invasion."

The sergeant nodded.

"The word is out, is it? That'll be Jack, of course."

"Tell me something I don't know," grunted Miller sourly. "Sorry Rookie, they've upset me down there."

Emboldened by this, the sergeant asked.

"What actually happened, though?"

The man behind the desk leaned back, rubbing his hand over eyes that seemed o be filled with sandpaper.

"Albert Westman—I never knew old Pop's name was really Albert, did you—?—"

"—No—"

"—well, it was. He'd been in the pub about an hour, about two hours, not very long, for quite some time. You can take a lovely choice from all these first-class witnesses. He was quite cheerful, a bit depressed, full of jokes, kept himself to himself. He left the pub alone, that's about the one thing they're all sure of. Nobody seems to know what time it was, except that it was before closing time. Could have been five minutes, could have been an hour. Anyway, another customer, Thomas Crabtree—"

"—I know him. He's harmless—"

"—left when the landlord called time. He stumbled across old Pop lying in the entrance to an alleyway just across the road. There was nothing he could do by himself, so he went back to tell Harry Edwards. Harry went out with a few others, and they carried the old man back into the pub, and then phoned us."

Sergeant Rook made a face.

"Very helpful," he muttered. "So there's no chance of picking up anything from the actual scene of the crime, not with all those great feet tramping about. Be a nightmare for Forensic. About like searching around Piccadilly Underground."

Miller nodded.

"You're right. Still, to be fair, I don't really blame them for what they did. There was no way of being sure the poor old sod was dead. Might have been just a bash on the nut for all they knew. Couldn't just leave him lying there."

"H'm. Pity though. What was it, robbery?"

The inspector sighed.

"I expect so. There was no wallet on him, just a few coins in one of his trouser pockets. Nobody seemed to know whether he even had a wallet."

Rook tutted irritably.

"Well, that's a lie for a start. Everybody knew he always carried one. Even I know that."

Miller looked at him with interest.

"What makes you so positive?"

"Because of Dandy Jack," was the reply. "You know how proud the old man was of Jack. He always carried this wallet, because it protected the photographs. The one of Jack in his boxing days. If any unwary stranger made any reference at all to the fight game, and even if he didn't, sometimes, Pop Westman would have those photos spread out on the bar, before you could say Henry Cooper."

The seated man inclined his head.

"Do you know, you're spot on there, Rookie. I'd forgotten that. Years ago, when I was new, I can

41

remember having that lot flashed at me. You're absolutely right. Thanks."

He made a scribbled entry in his notebook. The sergeant looked grave.

"Only confirms what you were saying though, doesn't it? I mean, they must have really put the shutters up down there. Not going to help much, is it?"

The inspector's next remark surprised him.

"I'm not too bothered about the locals, anyway. I've got a much bigger problem than them. It was music night in the lounge bar. Every Tuesday and Thursday. Brings in the mid-week trade. Anyway, there was a hundred plus in there last night. From all over. The leather boys, motor-bikes, everything."

"Christ."

This was bad news indeed. These youngsters would have come from all over, for that kind of do. If one of them had fixed old Westman, a difficult job was going to become almost impossible. There was no need for Sergeant Rook to make any comment, apart from the brief expletive. Both men knew the position without spelling it out. Instead, he changed the subject.

"Jack turned up, I suppose?"

"Oh yes, dear Jack was there. And his dancing partners, Georgie Parks and Big Bill Yateley. Good as gold, all of 'em. Very quiet."

"How did Jack take it?"

"He was very quiet, like I say. No fuss, no bluster. But I could feel waves coming out of him. D'you know what I mean? Nothing against me personally, or even policemen in general. Just contained anger, fury if you like. Somebody's going to suffer for this little lot. Jack's not the man to be buggered about, any time. But this—"

He left the sentence uncompleted, and there was silence for a few moments, each man busy with his private imaginings. Then he spoke again.

"By the way, did you put the feelers out on the O'Connells?"

Rook nodded.

"Yes, I did. They weren't hard to find, it seems. They had a private party going on in some rat-trap off Berwick Street. Place called the Red Cockatoo. Do you know it?"

Miller made a face.

"Come off it, Rookie. I hardly ever go up the other end, except for a meal now and then. Red Cockatoo? Never heard of it. It was probably the Red Monkey last week, and it'll be the Red Crocodile next week. These places open and shut so fast, it's a full time job for our local coppers to keep track of 'em, never mind some poor visitor like me. What was the party about?"

"I don't know. Both the O'Connells were there, couple of birds. And Maxie Bloom."

"Ah, yes. Mr Bloom. Another old chum. He must be due for some more nice porridge, surely? Been a couple of years, now."

"Three."

"Is it really? How time flies. That would be nice, wouldn't it? If we could get Dandy Jack and old Maxie arguing about tonight's little affair. Get 'em at each other's throats, then nick the pair of 'em for causing an affray. And carrying too, perhaps. Nice little deadly weapon charge."

The uniformed man grinned.

"That sounds like incitement, inspector. I'm sure you didn't mean it to sound like that."

"Tut tut, Rookie. How can you say such a thing? A police officer has to be alert for all signs of potential criminal activity. I'm just being alert, that's all."

"Or day-dreaming."

"No law against that. Especially after nearly twenty-four hours of consecutive duty."

He looked at his watch, yawning.

"More tea, inspector?"

"No thanks. It's not my stomach's fault I'm tired. No need to inflict unnecessary punishment. No, I'm going home. Is Inspector Fennimore cross with me?"

The sergeant shook his head.

"Not as cross as he might have been. There was a bit of a set-to at that warehouse job. He's got a couple of bruises to rub, so he's had plenty to think about."

Miller stood up and stretched.

"Well, I'll scribble him a little note, and then I'm off."

"Right. I'll be seeing you."

Cyril sat on his bed looking at the money spread out at his side. Sixty-three quid, he gloated. Not a fortune, true. But it was all his, he didn't have to share it with anybody. It was his first real job of work where he'd acted alone, and he felt elated. There could be a mint of money in this lark. Just think of all the hundreds of pubs in London. Thousands probably. If he could pull off a job like this every night, he'd be rolling in money. Just think. Sixty three pounds a night, seven nights a week, that would be—no, that was too hard. Make it sixty pounds a night—we'll put the odd three in the poor box—so, seven nights would be, seven sixes, that would be forty-eight was it? Forty four? Well, it didn't matter. It was over forty. That meant four hundred pounds a week. He grinned to himself, in the shadowed light from the bedside lamp. He was in the four hundred pound a week class, and that made him a big man by any standards. And cash in hand, don't forget. None of this income tax rubbish. Oh yes, he might well feel pleased with himself.

He'd have to move away, of course. Naturally. You

couldn't expect a bloke of his class to stay in this lousy neighbourhood. Up west, that's where he'd live. With some bird. Perhaps two birds. A bloke in his situation would have his pick. And a car, too. Big American car would be best. All that lovely chrome. Still, first things first. He'd have to pay off what he owned on the scooter. In the morning, he'd see to that. For a brief moment he recalled the argument with the old man. He'd been too soft with him, that had been the trouble. Wouldn't make that mistake again. Now he relived the scene.

"Let's have the wallet, dad, and don't make a fuss. Then you won't get hurt."

The old man had taken a step back, peering at him.

"You pissed, or what? Get out of my way."

Cyril produced a heavy-duty spanner.

"You're asking for it."

That would frighten him, surely. But it hadn't. The old man had come at him fast, swinging his fists. One of them caught Cyril on the side of his chin, taking him off balance. Anger overcame his own nervousness as he crashed the metal against the grey head.

"Take that," he snarled.

The old man had gone down without a sound. Cyril breathed heavily, rubbing at his jaw. Well, he did ask for it, and no mistake. Reaching inside the prone man's jacket he pulled out the wallet and slid it into a side pocket. Then, with a quick heave, he pulled his victim off the pavement and into the entrance to an alleyway. The street was dark and deserted as he hurried back to the carpark.

Now, seated on the bed, he passed a hand over his damaged jaw. Bit tender, that was all. Probably have gone down by the morning. He hoped it would, because he didn't want another inquisition from his mother. Still, it did hurt a bit. Who'd have thought the old geezer would have that much go in him? Anyway, and

Cyril grinned to himself maliciously, the old man would have a headache as big as today and tomorrow, when he came round. Serve him right, trying to chuck his weight about at his age.

Then he remembered he hadn't looked at the other contents of the wallet. All he'd done so far was to concentrate on the cash. Might be some cheques, or a credit card perhaps. But there was nothing. Just some old photographs. These showed a young man in various boxing attitudes, fully attired for the ring. So that was it. The old man must have done a bit in his time, that's what made him so quick with his hands. Looked as if he might have been a rough handful, too, in his day. Well his day was done.

At that time, Cyril had no way of knowing how accurate his last thought had been.

FIVE

The alarm went off at eight. Jan Stewart reached out
sleepily and switched it off. Lord, eight o'clock already.
She'd only been in bed about three and a half hours.
Let's see, what was today, Wednesday? Yes, Wednesday. Tuesday seemed to have gone on for ever, and even
when she'd finally been successful in getting Jack to
bed, she hadn't been able to sleep for ages. There was
too much going on inside her head. For Jan was in no
doubt that the next few days could well prove to be a
turning point in her life. Up to now, her relationship
with Jack Westman had been an entirely personal and
local matter. Only a few people knew of it, and they did
not include her own family. Her parents did their best
to keep their thinking along modern lines, but they
would be very resistant to her setting up house with any
man. If the man were acceptable in other ways, she

could probably have talked them round, in time. But there was nothing acceptable about the man she loved, not in their terms. They would classify him as little better than a gangster, she had no illusions about that. To top off everything else, Jack was a married man. Technically, that was. His unfortunate wife had suffered an irreversible mental breakdown some years before Jan met him, and Jack's existence was the one stable plank in her lost life. So, unless the poor woman was to die, Jack was not in the marriage market.

Jan knew well, and accepted, all these things. But there would be a change now. There would be newspapers and police officers and courtrooms. A five-minute wonder, from the news point of view. But that five minutes could have a serious and permanent effect on both of them.

"Was that the alarm? Already?"

Jack's sleepy grumble came from beside her.

"You go back to sleep," she instructed. "I'll wake you at ten."

"No," he countered. "Might as well be at it. Busy day. Make some coffee, there's a good girl."

She went into the kitchen, and set up the percolator. Behind her, she could hear him moving around.

"Coffee's ready," she called, seating herself at the breakfast bar.

He came in slowly, and it made her heart turn to see the strain on his face. But he managed a smile.

"Don't know what I'd do without you," he confessed.

"Well, it doesn't arise, does it. If you'd sooner not talk now—"

"No," he interrupted, "I must tell you, before the newspapers turn up. They're probably on their way now, I shouldn't wonder."

He told her what had happened, in short, clear

sentences.

"It might sound foolish, but I suppose the police have no idea who might have—"

Her voice tailed away as he shook his head grimly.

"Too early, yet. Besides, they've got a real job on their hands with this one. Not only have they got the locals to worry about, but the lounge bar was full of strangers. Come to listen to the band, you see."

Jan showed quickened interest.

"A band? You mean a group."

"A band, a group, what's the difference?"

She smiled.

"Quite a lot, actually. Now then, what kind of group is it?"

Jack felt a touch of impatience. What did it matter about the damned group? There were more important things to think about.

"I don't know," he shrugged. "What does it matter?"

"It could matter quite a lot," she told him seriously. "Bear with me, Jack. Did you notice what they call themselves?"

He sighed.

"Look here love, I know you're anxious to help and all that. But just tell me, what are you driving at?"

She leaned back, and when she replied her face was serious.

"Groups usually attach themselves to a particular style of music. And that style brings support from that section of the young community. So, for example, if they play punk music, the punks will follow them. And perhaps a few skins."

"Skins?" he echoed.

"Skinheads," she explained, "sometimes known as bootboys."

Jack nodded.

49

"So?"

"So, if you find out the style of music, you'll know two things. You'll have a rough idea of what kind of clothes the boys will wear, and you'll be able to find out where else they are likely to go to find their particular music."

Understanding began to dawn on his face.

"See what you mean. Instead of just looking for some young tearaway, who could be anybody, we cut down the numbers. Right?"

"Right."

"I like this. You mentioned punks. What other kinds are there?"

Jan considered, counting on her fingers.

"Well, there are the mods. Their music developed from something called New Wave. Then there are the soulies, who follow soul music, reggae and funk. After that—"

"Hang on," he interrupted, "I've heard of this reggae. That's the black boys isn't it? West Indians, and that?"

"Well, yes, they were the originators, but quite a lot of white youngsters follow it."

Jack waved a hand.

"Yes, yes, but it's mainly black. It would bring the black crowd to where they play it, no?"

"Yes, I'm sure that's true."

He seemed satisfied at that.

"We can forget that. Harry Edwards wouldn't risk bringing that lot down to the Hope and Anchor. A publican has enough trouble."

Normally a prejudiced statement of that kind would have been enough to stir Jan into an angry response, but at that moment she scarcely noticed it. Jack was already on his feet, and crossing to the telephone.

"You could be on to something here, Jan. Hang on a

minute." Then into the telephone, he said "Harry, this is Jack. Sorry about the time. That group of yours. What do they call themselves? The what? Blast Off? Are you sure?"

He looked over at Jan, shrugging. She nodded her head, whispering.

"Could be."

"All right, Harry. Now, what kind of music do they play? What? I know it's bleeding loud, it always is. But what kind of music? Well, there must be a poster up or something. Can't you have a look? Right." He raised his eyes to the ceiling for Jan's benefit, and waited. "Mod. You're quite sure about that? It says on the poster 'We are the Mods'. No, nothing special. Just an idea I had. Thanks, Harry. Yes, I'll be seeing you."

He replaced the receiver carefully.

"It's a mod group. Call themselves Blast Off. That's all he knows."

Jan found herself beginning to get excited.

"It's a good start, Jack. It'll give the police a much narrower field. They'll be able to concentrate their enquiries more effectively."

"Yes. Yes, that's right. Of course they will."

But he didn't sound very enthusiastic. The mention of the police had brought a cautious look into his eyes. At the moment Jan didn't understand the reason. She would remember the reaction later.

Jack sipped at his coffee. It was excellent, as always, but he was too busy with his own thoughts to notice. Jan was a great girl, certainly the most important female there had ever been in his life. She occupied a special niche in the scheme of things, a place apart from his outside activities. He kept the two worlds separated, and most successfully. This was his home, their place, and that was the way it must remain. When he tried to analyse his reasoning, as he had done many times, he

51

found it obscure and confused, but one thing was clear. Jan's whole upbringing and training had given her a view of the law which was poles apart from his own. To her, everything was quite straightforward. If the law was being broken, or if you were in some kind of trouble, you simply called the police station. They would send a nice friendly constable round, and he would go away and put everything straight. That was why we had policemen, wasn't it? In the daytime they directed traffic, and spent hours explaining to puzzled tourists the best way to get to Buckingham Palace. Then, by night, when all the responsible citizens were in their beds, the guardians of law and order waged war on the dark forces of crime. It was a very tidy concept, and it kept Jan happy.

The business now could change all that. Try as he might, Jack was very doubtful as to whether he could continue to keep his two worlds apart. Not until things were settled.

He cleared his throat.

"Listen pigeon, I've been thinking. I'm going to be very busy these next few days. In and out at funny times. On top of that I'm going to have a lot on my mind. I was just wondering whether you wouldn't be better off if you went and took some time off. Had a little break down by the sea, or something."

He avoided looking at her as he said it. He was afraid she'd look into his eyes and read his mind, as she was uncomfortably capable of doing sometimes. If she once suspected what his intentions were, he'd be in for more than an argument, and he knew it. A thing like this might even take her away from him, and that was something he refused to contemplate.

Jan heard the words, but mostly she looked at his face. Poor love. He didn't really understand her too well. Did he really think he could pack her off at a time like this?

"This is me you're talking to, my gambling friend," she told him gently. "I'm over here, if you'd care to look up. A genuine full-grown woman, not a pretty toy. I can't believe you're serious. Do you think for a moment I'm going to go off and leave you, at a time like this? Just when you really need me, when I'm really able to do something positive for you? Kindly drop the subject, and let's talk practicalities. Now, to start with, somebody's going to have to go down to your father's place. Look for his papers, and so forth. Would it help if I did that?"

It was clear from the determined set of her chin that there was no point in pursuing the idea. Jack knew that expression too well, and smiled, despite himself.

"Just thought I'd mention it."

"Well, you have. And it was a terrible idea, so let's forget it. Now then, what do you want me to do?"

Sandra Bowers opened her eyes reluctantly, then shut them again, yawning. What time was it? Oh, ten past eight. Not too bad. She could afford another five minutes in bed. No. Perhaps not. Last time she had an extra five minutes, she'd slept for an hour and a half. Old Mr Wilks had been doing his nut when she rolled into the supermarket at ten o'clock. Customers were clogging all the check-outs, and there was no doubt whose fault it was. It was hers. Didn't want to go through that again. Not because of the customers, sod them, but because of the way old Wilks could dress a girl down. In front of the others, too. That shouldn't be allowed, that shouldn't. He shouldn't be able to speak to her like that in public. Wouldn't happen in a car factory, she was quite sure. Cause a strike that would. Didn't take much, these days. She could just see it now, all the girls walking out, chanting 'Wilks must go'.

'Clean up our supermarkets'. Might even turn into a national strike. She lay in bed, visualising the end product of Wilks' scandalous behaviour. 'National Women's Movement demands Enquiry'. Something like that. She might even get herself on the telly.

"And now Miss Bowers, we'd like to hear your side of things."

And she'd tell them, and all. They might even ask what her hobbies were, like in Miss World. That was a laugh, that Miss World. Better looking girls than that lot on every bus.

Wouldn't be bad, though. She'd enjoy that.

"My hobbies are mountaineering, and studying to be a brain surgeon."

There was movement outside her door, and the sound of heavy feet clumping down the uncarpeted stairs. Her brother Cyril was off to work, then. Funny, him shoving off like that, last night. Bas said he was chasing some bird. Wonder how he got on? He was funny sometimes, Cyril. Not bad, though, as brothers go.

The front door slammed, and a moment later she heard the angry muttering of his motor-scooter. The coast was clear.

"And how do you remove unsightly hair, Miss Bowers?"

"I wait until me brother's out of the way, then I use his electric shaver."

Pushing back the bedclothes, she swung her feet down to the floor. Christ, it was cold. Bet Miss World never had to put her feet down on any stinking lino. Shivering, she moved along the passage, and opened Cyril's door.

Gawd, he was an untidy bleeder. Like a dosshouse, this was. Clothes all over the floor, the tin lid that served as an ashtray piled high with dogends and apple cores.

To look at Cyril when he was out, all smart and polished up, no one would ever guess what state he lived in. Disgusting. Hallo, what was that on the floor, half-hidden by a discarded sock. Looked like a photograph.

Bending down, Sandra plucked at the protruding corner. It was a photograph. Young fellow in his boxing gear. She stared at the aggressive face. What a lovely piece of man, she decided. Didn't look like one of Cyril's lot, not one that she'd seen, anyway. Look at those muscles. Be a waste of time trying to resist a bloke with muscles like that. She probably wouldn't want to, anyway, she decided. Lovely.

Funny though, Cyril having a picture of him, who-ever he was. Not exactly the athletic type, our Cyril. His idea of exercise was a quick scooter-ride between one pub and the next. Not this one. Lovely, he was. She'd keep a sharp eye out for him.

Reluctantly, she put the photograph back where she'd found it. Wouldn't do for Cyril to think she'd been poking about in his room.

Now then, where was that shaver?

SIX

Georgie Parks tipped four heaped teaspoons of brown sugar into his coffee cup, and stirred vigorously. On the other side of the cafe table, Big Bill Yateley watched him, and shuddered. How could he drink that? Liquid toffee that was. Not coffee at all.

"Going to be a busy day, young William."

Years before, they had compared notes, to find that Parks was four days older than his stablemate. Ever since then, his seniority had been a standing joke between them.

"Oh, it'll be busy, all right," agreed Yateley. "But I don't know what chance we've got, really. If it was one of them kids, I mean, they come from all over, don't they?"

"They do, my son. That's what I meant by 'busy'. If they did come from all over, that's where we're going to have to go isn't it? All over. Do you have any idea how big this town is?"

"Course not," responded his companion, with heavy sarcasm. "I've only lived here all my life."

Parks nodded. It hadn't been a serious question, anyway. More thinking out loud, really. Whatever Jack wanted doing, he and Yateley would do, no quibbling. But, in his mind, he was convinced they would be wasting their time.

"Hiding to nothing," he muttered.

"Eh?"

Big Bill hadn't heard him clearly, and it was just as well. He hadn't meant to voice the thought. Wouldn't do for Jack to get the idea his heart wasn't in the task ahead.

"Nothing. Oh here's Jack."

Nobody else in the place paid any particular attention to the newcomer. It was the regular meeting place for the three men at eleven each day. The news of Pop Westman's murder had arrived too late for inclusion in the morning papers, and had even missed the early issues of the evening press. Tomorrow would be different. Jack Westman would then be a focus of attention.

"Allo Jack," greeted Parks. "Sid, let's have another coffee over here."

Jack settled himself down, lighting a cigarette. The other two said nothing. It was not a day for trivial greetings.

"Ta, Sid."

Jack nodded to the man in the white apron who set a cup in front of him and went away.

"Had a bit of luck," announced Jack quietly. "We just might get onto this geezer through the music. It's a special sort."

Big Bill looked quickly at Parks, but Georgie refused

to meet his gaze.

"How do you mean Jack, special?"

"These kids," Jack explained. "They follow their own brand of music. It all sounds the same to us, all yelling and guitars. But it's not. It's all different. And they stick to their own. Like Scotch."

The listening men had been looking puzzled up to that point. Now, their faces cleared.

"You mean like, a man who's a Black Label man won't have a Dimple?"

Big Bill put the question for them both.

Jack nodded.

"Couldn't have put it better myself. See how it cuts down the odds?"

The odds were something about which neither man needed any instruction. They represented familiar ground. Even so, Parks remained doubtful.

"You're right there, Jack, I can see that. This is going to make a big difference. But they're still long odds, ain't they? I mean, where we might have been talking about ten million to one, we're now down to about one million. Am I right?"

Jack shook his head.

"No. I've been turning the odds over in my head, I reckon," and he looked at each man in turn, to emphasize the point, "I reckon the odds are down in the hundreds. Four or five hundred to one. Now then, that doesn't sound half as bad, does it?"

Big Bill drew in his breath.

"I must say Jack, this is going to make a big difference. You're right there."

It didn't strike him that he'd repeated George's words almost identically.

"Still and all, Jack," insisted Parks. "With them odds, there'll be a lot to do. I mean, don't get me wrong, but if this was racing we was talking about, when was

58

the last time a gee-gee came in at that sort of price?"

"Off hand, I would say never," Jack replied.

Satisfied that he had made his point, Georgie Parks nodded. Jack would have some more cards up his sleeve, he was sure of that.

Jack had worked out this conversation in advance, unknown to his henchmen. There was no doubt in his mind that there would be a tremendous effort involved in the enquiry he was about to launch. And, although he had no wish to dwell on the prospect, the chance of a successful outcome could only be slim, at best. That, however, was something for his private thoughts. If there was to be any hope at all of success, it could only come from a maximum effort on the part of everyone concerned. He wanted no doubts in anyone else's mind. The next move was to sell these two his programme. So far, it had gone well. He had brought them away from the amateur Sherlock Holmes atmosphere, and into a discussion about odds. They were on familiar ground now, and he could drive home his thinking.

"Now then, let's talk about five hundred to one. Suppose we could find some bookie daft enough to give us that price?"

"He'd have to be certified," stated Big Bill. "Not safe on the streets."

"True, but supposing," Jack insisted. "What would we do?"

Georgie Parks gave a short laugh.

"Might put a oncer on, just for a giggle. In case all the other horses dropped dead."

Then Big Bill piped up.

"Do better than that," he corrected. "Put a hundred on him, and nobble all the other runners."

Jack smiled, nodding. This was going well.

"Billie, my son, you are dead right. That is exactly what we are going to do."

59

The others widened their eyes. The pipedream of being on the inside with a big fix on a race was close to the heart of every gambler. Jack knew he had all their attention.

"Now then, let's take this kid, the one we're looking for. Have to have a name for him."

"That's easy," Georgie spoke at once. "At five hundred to one, he's got to have a leg missing, to say the least of it. The Three-Legged Kid, that's him."

Big Bill chuckled.

"That's nice, that is. The Three-Legged Kid. I like that."

Jack liked it too. Accepting their proposal would cement their interest. Besides, it wasn't bad.

"Right then. Now, all the runners in this race are called Mods. That's what the music is, mod. We've got to get among all these runners, and tell them we want the Three-Legged Kid to win. We are going to nobble everybody else in sight."

"That is going to cost a few bob," said Parks.

"A lot of money," agreed Yateley.

"You're right. I've got it, and I'll spend it. You can drop tens, twenties, fifties if you have to, I'm good for it. But the big prize is for the one who points the finger. The one who tells us where to find the Three-Legged Kid."

Georgie Parks leaned forward on his elbows, keeping his voice down to a minimum.

"How much are we talking about, Jack? How much is the big prize?"

Jack waited, for effect.

"One thousand pounds," he announced slowly.

"Blimey, was she wearing knuckledusters then?"

It was lunch-time in the works canteen, and the first time Bas had seen Cyril all morning.

Cyril grinned. He'd had so many remarks made about the bruise on his chin that he was no longer touchy about it.

"No," he denied. "What happened was I banged my chin climbing over her window-sill. Couldn't go through the front door, in case her old man was still up."

Bas nodded, not believing a word of it.

"Oh, yes. Worth a bit of a climb, was she?"

Cyril had also had an opportunity to think about the end of his story. If he made himself out to have had too much of a good time, he could have trouble later explaining why he didn't want to go back to that particular neighbourhood for a while. Much as it went against the grain, he could not claim great results with his mythical girl-friend.

He dropped his voice, looking around carefully before replying.

"I'll sort you if you ever repeat this, but the fact is I got nothing at all. Her old man started shouting up the stairs before I'd got going with her. Had to dive out the window again."

Basil's eyes widened. This didn't sound like Cyril at all. Maybe he was telling the truth after all.

"Straight up? You had to do a bunk?"

"Straight up," was the solemn reply. "But I'd deny it if you ever told anybody else."

His friend began to laugh.

"I don't think that's very funny," complained Cyril.

"Funny? It's a bleeding scream, that's what it is. There's you, the great lover, banging your face on the window, you're in such a rush. Next minute you're diving back out again. All for nothing."

He bent over his mirth. Cyril scowled, but was secretly pleased that his story was going over so well.

A new voice said.

"Hey, didn't you blokes say you was going to the Hope and Anchor last night? Listen to that group?"

Cyril turned at the interruption.

"Oh hello, Hec. Yeah, we was there. Nothing special. You didn't miss much."

Hec made a face.

"Not the music, no. I don't reckon that Blast Off. But what about the other, though? All the excitement. What did you see?"

Bas had stopped laughing now, and was following the exchange.

"What excitement?"

"It's in the paper. Look. You must have seen something."

Hec held out an early evening newspaper. On the front page, and slightly smaller than the headline, Bas read.

'Dunkirk Veteran Murdered'.

It was all about some old geezer who got bashed on the head and robbed outside the Hope the previous night. It seemed the victim was the father of the former light heavyweight contender Dandy Jack Westman. There was a lot of stuff about the old man, and a lot more about his once-famous son.

Bas had never heard of either of them, and was unimpressed.

"News to me," he shrugged. "Never happened while we was there. Coppers would have been all over the place. See, it says it happened late last night. We was gone by eleven. You see anything, Cyril?"

Cyril was standing slightly to Basil's right, and reading the article over his shoulder. A mistake. It must be a mistake. Or another old man altogether. That must be it.

"This Dandy Jack was quite a performer in his time," contributed Hec. "Old Smithie in the stores, he

62

remembers him well. He looks handy, I must say. There's a picture of him inside the back page. Ere, let me show you."

He riffled at the pages, while Bas retained the paper. Cyril felt as if he were watching a performance in a play. Nothing to do with him personally at all.

"Yeah, there it is, look."

A picture floated in front of Cyril's face. In one sickening second, he was brought back to reality. He'd seen the picture before. It was one of those he'd taken from the old man's wallet. Instinctively, his hand patted at an inner pocket.

Then he realised Bas had turned his head, and was looking at him.

"Well?" queried Bas.

"Well, what?" he countered.

"Well, did you see anything of this lot?"

"No. No, of course not. I was gone long before it happened. You know that, Bas."

His voice sounded strange, like that of a mechanical doll. His friend did not seem to notice.

"That's right," he confirmed. "Our Cyril had some bashing of his own to do last night. Right little darling, by all accounts."

Hec smiled.

"Oh yes. Bit you on the chin, did she?" Then, without waiting for a reply, he added "Oh, well, if you missed it all, you missed it. Just thought I'd ask."

Recovering his newspaper, he folded it carefully, and tucked it under his arm as he walked away.

"Near thing, that was," muttered Bas.

Cyril was alarmed at once. What was Bas getting at?

"How d'you mean, a near thing?" he demanded.

His tone caused his companion to flick his eyes round sharply.

"Missing all the fun over at that pub last night," he

explained. "What else would I mean? Blimey Cyril, you look terrible. You all right?"

It was true. Cyril's face had gone very pale, and his eyes were oddly bright. That bang on the chin might have done more harm than he knew. You read some shocking things about blood clots floating round inside you after a bang on the head.

Cyril swallowed, still struggling to regain his composure. He needed to think, needed to be left alone. All this was too much to take in, and the prospect of spending the rest of the afternoon at work was suddenly more than he could face. Bas was offering a way out.

"No," he said softly. "No, I don't feel too good. Tell you the truth Bas, I feel shocking. Got half a mind to go home."

"I should, if I was you. The place will probably fall down if you're not here, but don't worry about it. Tell you what, I'll ride along with you, if you like. Tuck you in, like."

That was something he certainly didn't want.

"No, ta. Be all right. Might get me head down for a couple of hours."

"Yeah, all right. I'll tell your foreman what happened."

"See you, then."

Cyril broke thankfully away. Ten minutes later he was riding out of the factory gates and heading towards home. On the way, he stopped at a newsagents to buy both the evening papers and a stock of cigarettes. There was an off-licence next door, and on a sudden simpulse he went in and bought a litre bottle of scotch. If he was going to have a day or two at home, he might as well make himself comfortable.

The house was empty, and he remembered that Wednesday was his mother's bingo day. That finished about four thirty, and she would go straight from there to her cleaning job at some nearby offices. That would keep her out of the way until about seven. His father and Sandra would be home first, between half past five and six. He had the place to himself for nearly five hours. Good.

In the privacy of his room, he poured out a large drink and swallowed it quickly. It made him cough, and tears sprang o his eyes. Silly really, he should have brought some water in. As he lit a cigarette, the lighter flame was shaking slightly.

Now he picked up the first newspaper, and began to read very carefully. There was no mistake. He'd known it all along, but the cold, factual descriptions left no room for any doubt. The other paper was the same. Just different words, that was all. It didn't change anything.

Suddenly his whole body began to shake. The lighted cigarette dropped to the floor, unheeded. A churning began in his stomach, and he knew he had to get into the bathroom before there was a disaster. In a clumsy, lumbering run he just managed to reach the lavatory before he was violently ill. Kneeling on the floor, his head held between clammy fingers, Cyril began to cry. Great racking sobs, that clawed deep into his vitals, producing further spasms of nausea.

He seemed to be in there for hours. Finally, exhausted and covered with cold sweat, he managed to heave himself to his feet. Leaning heavily on the washbasin, he ran water and began to splash it over his face. His inside was quieter now, and he felt utterly worn out. He reached out for a towel, and began to pat himself dry. When that was done, he turned to leave. There was a mirror facing him, and he compelled himself to look at his own reflection.

So that was what he looked like now.

Cyril Bowers. Murderer.

Funny, but he looked no different. Bit pale, but that

was because he'd been ill. Bruise on the jaw. Could happen to anybody. There was nothing on his face, except the bruise, that hadn't always been there. That was strange, that was. You'd think there'd be something. A look in his eye, a twist to the mouth. Something. But there wasn't. In an odd way, he found this comforting. If there was nothing showing on his face, it meant nobody could tell from just looking at him.

While he'd been riding through the streets, his mind had been busy examining possible routes of escape. He would go to some other big town, Birmingham, Glasgow, anywhere. Get himself some kind of a job, just enough to pay the rent, while he was waiting for his papers to go to Australia. Or Canada, perhaps. He'd have to use an assumed name, of course. All the police forces in the world would be on the alert for Cyril Bowers. Yes, he'd have to change his name all right. But then, he'd wondered. Wasn't there a lot of paper to fill in? Forms, and that? He seemed to remember when some distant cousin got a job abroad, there was a lot of talk about birth certificates and things. Load of bleeding red tape, that's all that was. Oh why hadn't he paid more attention at the time? If only he'd listened, he'd have known what he was up against, instead of scratching about in the dark.

Now, standing before the mirror, his mind began to clear. That was all panic, that was. He didn't have to do anything, go rushing off anywhere. Might have to later, that was true. But not now. The police weren't looking for him at all. Not Cyril Bowers, they weren't. Not him, personally. They were looking for some bloke who bashed an old man on the head. There were no witnesses, and they'd got a job on their hands. Mind you, it never paid to underestimate the coppers. Never mind all the jokes about the flat feet, and that. Clever bastards, they were. Most of the people who thought they were smarter than the law wound up in the nick. But they weren't miracle men. They needed time. And with this particular crime they were up against it, because they had a whole pub full of people to get through before they started getting interested in Cyril Bowers. Even if they ever did get interested. After all, he was a stranger to the district. Most of them were, that had been there last night. Take the police a fair old time to work their way through that lot.

Cyril's breathing was steadier now. He gave his face a final pat with the towel, and went back into his bedroom. There was an unpleasant smell, and smoke in the room. He must have dropped a cigarette, although he couldn't remember. He found it quickly enough, where it had dropped onto a discarded sock which was smouldering away. Clearing up the damage kept his hands and mind busy for the next few minutes.

After he'd cleaned up, and put the rubbish in the dustbin outside the back door, he went back into his bedroom. The first thing he noticed was the photograph lying by the bed. It must have been underneath the offending sock, he realised. Bloody lucky, that was. He'd been stupid and careless to drop it. Must have slipped out when he was replacing papers in the old man's wallet.

Bending down, he picked up the photograph and looked at it. He'd been wrong, then. It wasn't the old man in his early days at all. It was his son, the one they called Dandy Jack Westman, whoever he might be. Let's have another look at those newspapers.

SEVEN

Dave O'Connell stirred and moaned. Something terrible was happening, and there was this awful noise in his head. Gradually, his mind cleared, as sleep receded and reality took over. But the noise was still there.

Hammering. That's what it was. No, wait. The door. Somebody was pounding on the door. Kicking it too, by the sound of things. With growing consciousness came recognition, superseded at once by resentment.

Some saucy bleeder was banging on their door. Actually banging. Dave sat up abruptly, and was rewarded with a sharp ache at the base of his neck. Gawd, he must have sunk enough booze last night to float a ship. What time was it? The diamonds inset around his watch-face flashed brilliantly into his un-welcoming eyes. A quarter to one. It couldn't be. Not a quarter to one. He and his brother never stirred before two, and after last night's little lot, they'd promised themselves a lie-in.

Now here was this bleeding racket at the door.

Right.

He swung his legs off the bed, and creaked warily upright. There was no doubt about it. Dave me boy, today we feel shocking. The sight of the interior of the flat did nothing to restore his spirits. Over a hundred quid a week they paid for this place, him and Des, and still it always looked like a pigsty.

At the front door, he put out one hand to steady himself, and with the other slid back the securing bolts. He opened the door half an inch. Outside stood the immaculate and unsmiling figure of Max Bloom.

"Thought you was dead," greeted Max.

"Jeez, Max, what's the bleeding idea? Waking a man up in the middle of the night."

Dave stood aside to let the newcomer in. Max walked past him, staring around unfavourably, and wrinkling his nose.

"Blimey, you had an earthquake in here? There was nothing on the news."

Dave flopped into the nearest chair.

"Got a fag, Maxie?"

Bloom passed him a cigarette and lit it for him.

"Where's Des? Gone out for his morning run, has he?"

"Des is asleep, and if you've any Christian charity in you, you'll leave him there."

Max smiled. He'd a lovely smile, that Max.

"Christian?" he echoed. "You have to be joking, my old Davie. Can't think what the rabbi would say, if he heard you."

He was familiar with the inside of the place, and now walked over to open Desmond's door. Although the heavy curtains were drawn, he could make out the shape of a girl's head on the pillow, next to the unconscious Des. Max went inside, twitching back the covers.

"Wake up, darling. There's a producer outside from Paramount Pictures. Wants you for his star, he says."

She was bound to call herself an actress. They all did. The girl stretched, yawned and opened her eyes. Then she sat up.

"Who are you? What are you doing here?"

"I'm from Television Advertising," he assured her solemnly. "We're doing a coffee commercial. Piss off out in the kitchen, and start making some. Make a lot of it."

The girl snorted.

"You can't come in here, bossing me about—oh—"

She stopped talking as a hand swung stingingly across her cheek.

"I'm doing another one after this. It's on face surgery," Max told her. "You can be in that one, if you like."

Thoroughly frightened now, the girl scrambled to her feet, completely naked.

"Not bad," nodded Max. "Not bad at all. But right now, what we want is coffee."

While she was scrambling into some clothes, Max pulled aside the thick curtains. Des was hunched on his side, in a half-circle, only his wiry thatch of hair visible above the bedclothes.

"Come on now Desmond, out you get."

Max yanked at the eiderdown, pulling it clear of the sleeping man. Blimey, there was another one. A second girl was sound asleep on Desmond's other side. He began shaking at the pair of them.

Outside, Dave sat smoking, and waiting for the fog in his head to clear away. A girl stepped out from Des's room, and Dave stared at her, trying to remember. Gloria, was it? She was saying something.

"I said, where's the kitchen?" she repeated.

He pointed vaguely, and she went away. There was some angry rumbling behind her, and he realised Des was waking up. Max came back to join him, and another girl appeared in the doorway. No, that one was Gloria. The other one must have been—er—oh, the hell with it.

Max came and sat near him. They could hear Des stumbling around and cursing. Soon he emerged, rubbing a powerful hand over his face as if to chastise any lingering sleep.

"Did you let this maniac in?" he demanded.

Dave shrugged, and didn't bother to reply.

"I need a drink," announced Des, prowling around. "There must be one here somewhere."

"Girls are making coffee," Max said, to no one in particular.

"And you know where they can stick it," Des told him nastily.

He located a whisky bottle, with an inch or so remaining in the bottom, and tilted this against his lips. Then he shuddered.

"That's better. That is much better," he breathed. "Now then Max, what's the idea, getting here before the milkman?"

Max waved a hand.

"I don't think you boys will want those birds listening to our little chat. Business, this is. Confidential business."

The two brothers exchanged a glance. It would have to be something good, for Max to wake them up.

"How long's that bleeding coffee going to be?" shouted Des.

"Just coming," called one of the girls.

71

The one called Gloria—or was it the other one?—
came into the room, carrying a tray.

"I've put the milk and sugar separate," she
explained. "Didn't know who took what."

"Shove it down there, darling, and piss off."

Des pointed to a table.

"We haven't had any ourselves, yet," she protested.

"There's a coffee shop down the road. You and—
er—both of you. Out. Dave, you got the price of a
coffee for these little darlings?"

The other girl now stood beside her friend. This was
always a tricky moment for them. They never knew
quite what to expect. They knew about the evenings.
And the nights. Very predictable, both. But the
mornings were uncertain.

Dave opened a drawer, grumbling.

"Don't see why I should give 'em anything. You had
the pair of 'em. Nearly died of cold, I did, in there on me
own."

"I like that," protested the blonde one. "I spent half
the night trying to wake you up. Like being with a
corpse, it was. I had to go where I could be appreciated
in the end."

Des snorted with pleasure. Of the two, Dave was
more the ladies' man. But here he was, with two of them
to wave about, and Dave was nowhere. Good for his
image, this was. And in front of a witness, too.

"Quality talent this is, Davie. Too rich for the likes of
you. They needed a real man, eh girls?"

The two girls smiled, but kept a wary eye on the
discomfited Dave. He extended a twenty pound note,
and the nearest girl took it.

"Thanks very much."

Dave was prepared to leave it at that, but Des was
beginning to feel expansive.

"Don't be such a mean sod, little brother. There's

72

two of 'em, you know. Coffee's a terrible price these days."

Dave reluctantly held out a second note.

"That's it, girls. Out," he said flatly.

"Don't forget, Des, any time you feel like a nice evening," one of them began, but Dave interrupted.

"If you're still here by the time I count ten, you go out with nothing," he proclaimed nastily. "Sweet Eff A."

The girls skittered around like frightened rabbits, and were quickly gone.

The brothers looked at Max.

"All right Maxie, we're on our own. What's this big news?"

He looked at each in turn, savouring the moment before replying.

"Dandy Jack's got his wallet out," he announced finally. "Cash prize, no questions asked."

"Has he now?" queried Dave.

"How much?" Des asked.

Max spread his fingers wide apart in the air. When he told them, he emphasised each word separately.

"One—thousand—notes."

"A thousand pounds?"

Superintendent Myers repeated the words, and looked sharply at Sergeant Rook, who had just relayed the information.

"Yes, sir."

"I suppose your grass is reliable?"

The super felt he had to ask the question, although he knew in advance it was no more than rhetorical. Sergeant Rook was too old a hand to come in to his office wasting time with tittle-tattle.

The sergeant was not offended.

"The buzz didn't come in from a grass, sir. I've had it from two different sources. A newsagent down in Park

Road, and a bartender in the Grapes. I've no doubt there'll be more, as patrol officers report in."

"H'm."

A thousand nicker. That would stir a lot of memories, all right. People would find themselves calling to mind little details they'd forgotten. Or thought they'd forgotten, until they started rubbing ten-pound notes over the affected area.

"All right, Sergeant. Thanks for letting me know. Keep a log of all the places we hear about this. Like to get some idea of how wide this particular net gets thrown."

He knew the answer to that one, too. People talked about the way the African drums spread news far and wide. Well they were amateurs, compared to the way the grapevine operated in his part of the world. By the time the pubs opened that evening there wouldn't be a man, woman or child for miles who didn't know the story.

Pushing a key on the small intercom on his desk, he barked.

"Inspector Miller? You there?"

The box crackled back at him.

"Miller, sir."

"Come in, please, inspector."

Switching off the machine, the superintendent tilted his head back against his chair, whistling tunelessly, and drumming thick fingers against the desk top. This investigation was complicated enough already. Sergeant Rook's unwelcome news wasn't going to help.

Miller came in quickly, a folder of papers in his hand.

"Sit down, Touchy. You've heard the good news?"

The inspector wasn't going to be caught like that. It was an old dodge of the super's that. An unwary person could easily respond by trotting out some titbit that he wasn't yet ready for the super to know.

74

Carefully, he said.

"Lots of news about, sir. Don't know that I'd call any of it especially good."

Myers dropped his head forward to look Miller in the eye. Crafty sod.

"The reward, inspector," he explained. "Dandy Jack Westman has laid a thousand pounds on the table, for the man who puts the finger on the one who killed his father. Every copper in London knows about it, apparently. Don't tell me the investigating officer's been left out?"

Miller shook his head.

"Oh, no," he denied, "I've heard about it of course."

"Ah. Well, that's a relief. Did it cross your mind at all that I might be interested to share that information?"

The inspector thought quickly. He'd just seen the station sergeant leaving the super's office.

"I was on my way to tell you, just now" he countered, "but Sergeant Rook was in with you."

"I see. Well, it's bad news, Touchy. Have you had a chance to talk to Jack about it?"

"Not yet, sir. It's only just come in."

Myers banged lightly on the desk, and a pencil jumped in the air.

"Bad news," he repeated. "I don't like rewards, at any time. They bring heaps of duff information, waste the time of police officers, following up useless leads. You know all that as well as I do. I needn't go on about it."

"But they often work in the end," Miller pointed out. "Not many rewards go unclaimed."

"I know that," retorted his superior huffily. "But it doesn't make me like them any better. People getting paid for doing no more than their plain duty as citizens. It's all wrong."

The inspector kept quiet. This was an old hobbyhorse of the super's, and there was nothing to be gained by arguing with him. Realising that he wasn't going to provoke any further discussion, the superintendent spoke again.

"All wrong," he repeated. "Still, what you say's true. When all the smoke's cleared away, we've usually got a nice villain tucked up in his bunk. That's with a proper reward situation. When the money is posted by insurance companies, big firms and the like. When we have posters outside all the nicks. Proper legitimate ways of procedure. All that. Because all these legitimate people are trying to help us get information. Us. The forces of law and order, inspector. The people who are in business to catch villains. You and me. Have we got a situation like that now?"

Miller shook his head regretfully.

"No sir," he admitted.

"No sir," mimicked his chief. "No sir, we bloody do not. We've got a different situation altogether. Precisely the opposite, in fact. We've got money, cash money, and no question asked, being touted around the streets, in the pubs and cafes, all over. And what is the message? The message is, if you know anything about this murder, don't waste your time telling the police about it. Oh, no. You'll get nothing from them. Bring your nice information round to Mister Flash Bleeding Harry, Dandy Sodding Jack Westman, and he'll give you money. Try to imagine you're not a copper for a minute, and you have a little piece of news. Where are you going to take it, eh? Where?" Without waiting for a reply, Myers ploughed on, "You're going to take it to the friendly man with the five pound notes, right? Even if you don't help him much, Jack'll see you right. The very least you'll get out of it is a large scotch for your trouble. Correct me if I'm wrong, inspector."

Miller sighed.

"I wish I could, sir. What you've been describing is exactly what we're going to be up against. What's worrying me most about it, is the end of the line. Dandy Jack's not going to all this trouble to help us catch this murderer."

The superintendent nodded heavily.

"That's it, inspector. That is precisely it. Mr Bleeding Westman is going to gather up all his little pieces of information, that should be coming in here, to you. Then, when he's satisfied he's on the right track, he'll go out and crack a few skulls, just to eliminate the innocent. When he's put the frighteners on enough people, he'll know the man he's after. From then, it's a very simple matter. Our Jack fixes himself a nice alibi, slips out one dark night, and cuts the bastard's throat. You will correct me if you think any of my reasoning is faulty?"

He stared uncompromisingly at the hapless inspector. There was no answer to the superintendent's logic, and he knew it.

"Wish I could, sir. But I'm quite sure you're right."

Myers nodded.

"Course I am. We both know that. You might even find some police officers who would say 'Well, so what? If they cut each other's throats, it saves the time and effort of honest coppers.' Well, I'm not one of those people, Inspector Miller. I'm not having my nick, my officers, being by-passed by some back street imitation Robin Hood. The place for this murderer is in my cells, and it's your job to put him there. Crack down on this Westman. If he is withholding information pertinent to this murder enquiry, nick him. Keep on his back the whole time. That's all."

The inspector stood up and made for the door.

"Oh, and Touchy—"

The superintendent's voice made him pause in the

open doorway.

"—no vendettas. No little private fights. I know you're no particular mate of this Westman's, but play it absolutely according to the book."

"Yes, sir."

"And keep me informed the whole time."

"Right, sir."

When the door was closed, Superintendent Myres continued to stare at it for long seconds.

"Poor sod."

There was no one present to ask whether he referred to the man Jack Westman was looking for, or to the departed inspector.

EIGHT

The shift hooters grated their hollow message, and crowds of men began to stream through every doorway on the Watling Brothers compound. The eight feet tall steel gates were already wide open, security guards standing at either side to regulate the flow if it became necessary.

On the street outside, two men stood waiting, and scanning the emerging faces. One nudged the other and indicated with his head. They waited as a short wiry man approached, carrying a small attache case.

"Mr Barnes, is it?"

The man stopped, looking at them suspiciously. They were strangers, and he didn't like that. Strangers usually meant trouble.

"Who're you?" he demanded.

The taller of the two smiled.

"Friends of yours would like a word, if you don't mind. Mr Westman."

Barnes brightened at that.

"Dandy Jack? Where is he?"

The short man pointed.

"Just round the corner. Got a car round there. He would appreciate a couple of minutes, if you don't mind."

Barnes hesitated. That was twice they'd said 'if you don't mind'. Shouldn't be anything wrong, really. Besides, and he looked all round at his fellow workers as they hurried past, the place was too crowded.

"Yeah, all right."

There was a big Rover parked in the next street. He could see Dandy Jack leaning out of the window and waving to him.

"Hallo, Jack. How are you?"

"Hallo, Ernie. Nice to see you. You all right for half an hour?"

Of course he was all right. Tea was never before half past five, when his son got back from his office job.

"Sure," he confirmed. "No problem."

"Get in then, my son, and we'll have a chat. See you later."

This last remark was addressed to Ernie's escorts, who walked away and climbed into a Cortina further up the road. Jack opened the passenger door beside him, and Ernie got in.

"Nice motor," he said appreciatively. "Business is good, eh Jack?"

Jack smiled.

"You know how it is. Make a few bob, lose a few. Mustn't grumble."

Ernie Barnes and himself were old stablemates from the boxing days. The little man had showed some promise as a flyweight for a while, but he couldn't control his weight, and the essential speed and agility eluded him. He'd hung around for a year or two outside the ropes, acting as a second or a sparring partner, then gradually drifted away from the game altogether. They seldom met nowadays, their worlds being poles apart, but they retained the mutual affection men sometimes do from their youthful days.

The last time they had been together was a few months earlier, at a charity dinner for the St Mark's Boys' Club. This was an annual event, and was well supported by former members like themselves, who liked to sit around and swap yarns over a few drinks. In fact, on that occasion Ernie had gone at the bottle rather hard, and started talking more than he should have done. There was no harm in talking to Jack, because he was someone Ernie could trust, but if the wrong people had overheard him, it might have got him into some trouble.

Ernie was an electrician now, working at the Watling Brothers component factory. In the previous couple of years, no less than seven different attempts had been made to burgle the site, and each one had ended in disaster. This was because of the famous security arrangements at the factory, and Ernie was rather inclined to boast about these, because as one of the senior electricians he knew quite a lot about the systems.

"Impregnable," he would proclaim. "That's the word. Impregnable. You couldn't get into that place unless you had a tank, at the very least. Then you'd have a good chance of getting electrocuted. Plus the noise, of course. You can stand on me. That place is impregnable."

No one would argue with him. The facts spoke for themselves. Every time a bunch of villains took it into their heads to burgle the place, they came to grief. Ernie was right.

But that night, at the boys' club dinner, Ernie had suddenly begun to chuckle at some private joke. People had been telling blue stories, and it was naturally assumed that the little man had remembered a choice specimen.

"Come on Ernie, don't keep it to yourself."

"Let's all have a giggle."

But he was not to be drawn, and the others soon lost interest, when another guest asked if they'd heard the one about the parrot who could sing opera.

Jack had lost interest along with his fellow-members, but later still, when Ernie had consumed three or was it four more brandies, he turned to Jack suddenly and whispered in his ear.

"Could make this lot sit up, if I wanted to."

Dandy Jack was not a drinking man. Two glasses of wine, perhaps three on special occasions like this, and that was his limit for one evening. Scrambled wits and gambling do not make good bedfellows, and Jack always liked to keep a point or two in front of everyone else. Ernie was well-oiled, and had been for the previous hour at least. This was the stage of an evening when Jack was getting monumentally bored, and looking for an excuse to leave.

One thing he did not want at that moment was to listen to a lot of maudlin confidences, even from an old mate like Ernie Barnes.

"Sure you could Ernie," he soothed. "I know that. Have another cigar."

Ernie was affronted.

"You think I'm pissed," he accused.

"No, no, Ernie. Nothing of the sort. We're all having a nice friendly drink, that's all."

The menu had been typed on white cards, and slotted into silver-plated holders along the dining table. Ernie now reached out for the nearest of these, narrowly avoiding knocking down a neighbour's glass.

"Scuse me," he muttered.

He lifted out the card and placed it face down on the table, between Jack and himself. Then, fishing in his pockets, he produced a small stub of pencil. This was going to be one of those drawing jokes, decided Jack.

Ernie drew lines on the card, biting at his lips and screwing up his eyes in the enormous concentration required to maintain control of the pencil. Then he prodded Jack with his elbow, and dropped his voice to a barely audible level.

"Say this is the firm," he pointed to the rough semblance of an oblong. "Here, here and here, those are the entrances, right? Oh, and here too. You with me?"

"Certainly, Ernie. But what about it?"

The little man blinked owlishly around, to be certain they were not being overheard.

"People keep trying to burgle the place, you know."

He made his announcement with deep solemnity, as though divulging some state secret. But, despite himself, Jack became interested. Ernie wasn't going to all this trouble simply to tell him something that was public news.

"Yes, I know," he returned. "Come unstuck though, don't they? Burglar alarms, and all that."

Ernie smiled knowingly, and tapped at the side of his nose. The pencil in his hand made a black smudge.

"And all that," he echoed. "They've tried the front, that's here, four times. Twice they've tried that door there, and that one once. No chance."

He had made small marks to indicate the entrances at which the failed attempts had been made. There was still one doorway unmarked. Thinking he could foresee what was coming, Jack said, pointing with his finger.

"But not that one, eh? Are you saying they might

have done better over there? Is that it?"

Ernie clapped him on the shoulder, winking heavily.

"Stands to reason they'll try that one next. I mean, it stands to reason, dunnit?" He chuckled. "I'm waiting for that. That entrance there, it's the worst of the lot. Not only do you set off every bell except the gate-keeper's alarm clock, you got your nice photograph taken as well. No extra charge. All part of the service. Good, innit?"

Jack felt slightly let down. All that Ernie was saying was that Watling Brothers was no-go for the break and enter squad. Everybody knew that already.

"Very impressive," he said drily. Then a further thought struck him. "It all relies on the electrics, though, doesn't it? You're one of the chief electricians. I'll bet you could nobble it, if you wanted to. Pull out a fuse, cut a wire or two. None of the systems would work then, would they?"

His companion took another sip at his brandy, shaking his head sadly at the same time.

"They've thought of all that. We check each other's work all the time. And we have to sign to show we've done it. Even if one of us managed to cause some damage like that, and it wasn't noticed, they wouldn't have any trouble finding out which bloke it was. The signature, see? They'd have the signature. The system is foolproof, mate. Worked out by some real clever bastard, that was."

So the whole conversation was pointless, after all. Disappointed, Jack leaned back.

"Well, there you are then."

Ernie chuckled.

"No, listen a minute. Listen. Not finished yet. Do you know what's over there?"

He pointed with the pencil to a spot outside the oblong. Jack tried to visualise the site, but he wasn't sufficiently familiar with the neighbourhood.

"Give up," he shrugged. "You tell me."

"Substation, that's what."

"What's that, then? Railway, you mean?"

The little man was aggrieved.

"Course not. Substations don't mean bleeding railway stations. Electricity. That's what it is. Belongs to the electricity board."

"So?"

"Come closer a minute."

Reluctantly, Jack craned his head forward so that it almost touched Ernie's.

"That's where they should put the boot in," whispered Ernie. "No problem at all. You knock that place out, and everything inside the firm is dead. Alarms, photo-electrics, doorseals, the lot. It all works on power, you see. Take the power away, and it's all useless. Load of scrap. Now do you see?"

Well, well. So there really had been something worth waiting for, after all.

"Are you sure about this?" queried Jack.

His old friend was instantly aggrieved.

"Sure? Course I'm sure. What are you saying, I don't know me job, or something?"

"Of course not. Keep your hair on, Ernie. Listen, you could make a nice tickle there, if you took this to the right people."

Ernie heaved his shoulders.

"I know that. Tell you the truth, Jack, I've thought about it. Quite a lot, actually. But I'd be afraid. I know one or two likely customers who'd be very interested, I know. But nobody I could really trust. No, I'd wind up with the shitty end, I'm quite sure. Two years hard, me job gone, and everything. The rest of them over in Spain or somewhere, getting pissed in the sunshine, and laughing their heads off at that mug, Ernie Barnes."

Jack nodded, relieved.

"Very wise, my son. Have another drink, and forget it. Waiter."

Now, looking at the smiling man beside him, Jack said.

"You were a bit under the weather when I left you last time. D'you remember, the annual booze-up for the Boys' Club?"

Ernie grinned ruefully, patting at his head.

"I remember," he acknowledged. "My head remembers too. I was still bombed out most of the next day. Good do, though."

Jack nodded.

"Yes. They made nearly two thousand quid that week for the club, altogether. Drop in the ocean really. Money don't go far these days."

"That's right enough. Time I've paid the missus, and a couple of the old H.P.s, I don't have a lot to chuck about. Still, there's a big rise in the pipeline. Twenty per cent, we're asking for. Can't see it coming off. Might get twelve or fourteen though, with a bit of luck. Be nice, that would."

"Hope you get it. Tell me, did you ever think any more about the chat we had that night? At the do?"

"Chat?" Ernie's face was perplexed. "Tell you the truth, Jack, it's all a bit vague after about half past nine. What did we talk about? Jog me memory."

"All sorts. About your job, mostly. You seem to be quite well in, over at Watlings."

The little man was embarrassed.

"Got a bit boring, did I? Sorry about that."

"No, no," he was assured. "Far from it. I found it very interesting. Course, as you say, you were a bit over the odds. Probably exaggerated a bit."

"About what?"

Jack turned his head away before replying.

"Oh, all sorts of things. Let's think, now. The security system, that was one thing."

Ernie's tone was alarmed, as he said.

"Security? What about it?"

The man beside him now looked directly into his face.

"About how it can be by-passed."

"By-passed?" Ernie averted his gaze. "I never said that, surely? Must have been stoned out of me mind. It's impossible, you see."

"No."

The word was flat, positive. Ernie's mind began to race, churning desperately through the memory fog surrounding the evening of the boys' club dinner. Jack was talking again.

"No, it's not impossible, Ern. It can be done. From outside. The main power comes in from this electricity substation."

"Substation?" repeated his listener, thoroughly nervous now.

"You told me all about it. Even drew me a little plan, pissed as you were."

Gawd, he hadn't told him that, surely? No, no. He would never have told him that. Ernie made one final attempt at denial. He laughed, a hollow, unconvincing sound.

"I must have been drunker than I thought. Making up a yarn like that. Still, as you say, I'd certainly had a skinful."

"Yes, you had," confirmed his interrogator. "Only you didn't make it up, at all. And it wasn't a bad little drawing, considering how shaky your hand was. Gave the position of the substation and everything. I've been over there, old chum. Seen it for myself. It's there, all right."

There was no further protest. Ernie sat quite still,

staring out of the car, and wishing hopelessly the whole conversation was a dream. Jack was silent for a few moments. The rest of this discussion would follow predictable lines now. His old boxing companion would realise that, left to himself. After a while, he began again.

"You interested me, with your little theory. Then, I thought to myself, 'Ah, it sounds all right. But, with all due respect, Ernie's only an electrician. Might be a bit more to it than he thinks.' So what do you suppose I did?"

Ernie shook his head miserably.

"What?"

"I went to have a little chat with a man I know. Very respectable man, very straight. Proper electrical engineer, he is. What they call chartered."

The man in the passenger seat widened his eyes.

"You told him? About Watlings?"

"You must think I'm soft in the head. No, of course not. I spun him a yarn. Want to know what it was?"

Ernie nodded. Anything. He would sooner talk about anything, other than what he knew must inevitably come.

"I said there was this firm I was thinking of investing in. You know, buying a few shares. Everything worked by electricity, and I was a bit bothered because it seemed to me everything relied on this one substation. Suppose something happened to it, I asked him? All the processes would stop, raw materials would get damaged. All that. He told me something very interesting. He said a place should have an alternative, and that was the first thing I should check. Two main ways of dealing with it, according to this man. Either there would be another source of supply, in other words another substation. Or, there ought to be an emergency generator, inside the place. It made good sense to me.

What's the answer?"

The little man licked at lips which were suddenly dry.

"He's quite right about that. There should be one or other of those things. But there isn't, you see. That's the whole point. There isn't."

Jack nodded thoughtfully, careful to keep the triumph he felt from showing on his face.

"Well now, Ernie, it seems we're going to have a little chat about Watling Brothers. And stop looking so worried. The way I've got all this worked out is not going to do you any harm. In fact, old mate, you are going to touch for a nice few bob. Now, listen."

The instruction was unnecessary.

Ernie was listening very carefully indeed.

NINE

It was five twenty five in the afternoon. Harry Edwards walked around all the bars in the Hope and Anchor, checking for tidiness. Tonight would be like a Christmas Eve, he knew that. All his regulars would be in without fail, and on top of that would come the sightseers. People who wanted to see for themselves the pub where a murder had been committed. Well, all right, it hadn't been in the pub, but it was practically outside the door.

Yes, it was all looking very nice, he decided. The early birds would include all the customers who'd been in the saloon bar during the latter part of the previous evening. Dandy Jack Westman had spread the word that he would appreciate a chat with them, and they wouldn't need to be told twice.

"All right," Harry called out. "Open the doors."

From every bar there was the sound of heavy brass bolts being drawn. Blimey, they must have been waiting outside on the pavement. A trickle of customers appeared at once.

"Evening, Harry."

As he began to pull up the first pint of the evening, Harry saw a tall, attractive blonde girl appear in the doorway. Not the usual run at all. Bit snooty, if anything. Reporter, most likely. She'd never been in before, he wouldn't have forgotten this one. Ah, she was coming towards him.

"Good evening, are you Mr Edwards?"

"That's right, miss. Shan't keep you a minute."

He carried the foaming pint away. She'd be a gin and tonic, this one. Plenty of ice and lemon. Or could be a vodka, these days. Fashions change. Harry put money into the till, and went back to where she was standing.

"Now then, miss. What can I get you?"

She smiled, and it was a nice warm experience.

"I'm Jan Stewart," she told him. "A friend of Jack Westman's. I'm to meet him here."

Jack's bird. Of course, that's who she was. Harry had heard about the girl, but dismissed most of the chat as being unreliable. Privately he had decided she would be no different from any other brass, once you actually saw her. And now that she was actually here, he knew just how wrong he had been. Jack had said he was to look out for her.

"Pleased to meet you," he assured her. "Jack said he'd be in early. Can I get you a drink while you're waiting?"

"Thank you. Could I have a bottle of lager, please?"

Lager. That was a turn up.

Jan took her drink and went across to sit at a table while she waited. It was surprising to her to see how many customers were out drinking at this hour. Mostly on the elderly side too, she noted. Some of these men must have known Jack's father, and she could visualise how easily he would merge into one or other of the small groups which were beginning to form. Another thought struck her. There were probably one or two people here who would remember Jack as a child. It would be interesting to ask them about that. Perhaps the old boy in the smartly pressed blue suit.

Where was Jack, anyway? He'd said five thirty, and he must know she wouldn't relish sitting around by herself in a public house. A strange pub, at that. Jan's day had been rather wearing. An endless procession of grimy offices, registering the fact of his father's death, and all the procedures that flowed from it. She'd especially hated the funeral place, with its air of professional solemnity and the tired-looking rubber plants.

Each time the door opened she looked across with interest. It was almost a quarter to six when she recognised the latest new arrivals. They were Jack's constant companions, Georgie Parks and Big Bill Yateley. Jan inclined her head in recognition. The two men nodded back, Yateley smiling at the same time.

"What's she doing here?" he wondered.

"Waiting for Jack, I spect," muttered Parks.

"Hadn't we better buy her a drink, or something?"

"No," ruled his companion, flatly. "She's already got a drink. Anyway, Jack says no mixing, and he's right. Oil and water."

They walked across to where the landlord was standing.

"'Allo, 'Arry. Jack's not here yet then?"

"Hallo gents. No, not yet. What you gonna have?"

Big Bill Yateley began to reply, but Georgie cut him off.

"Too early," he decided. "And it's going to be a long night. Where's the band bloke?"

Harry jerked a thumb to his right.

"Waiting for you in the lounge bar. The messenger boys are there, too."

Parks was pleased.

"Nice going, Harry. You musta been busy."

Harry shrugged.

"The Westmans are old friends and customers. Glad to be able to do something useful."

He was not convinced, privately, that Dandy Jack's scheme was going to work. The idea was to reproduce Tuesday night's events on Thursday. Jack would pay for the group, Blast Off, and as many as possible of the people who attended on the night of his father's murder would be rounded up to form the audience. Admission would be free, and drinks would be on the house, for the whole evening.

When Dandy Jack Westman explained the idea to him earlier that morning, Edwards had been frankly sceptical.

"The band's easy enough, and my side of it," he granted, "but the crowd? How will you ever contact that lot? Nearly all of 'em were strangers to me. I wouldn't know where to start, Jack."

Jack smiled.

"You're wrong there, Harry. You do know where to start. And I'm hoping that's all we'll need. You know some of those kids, don't you?"

"A handful, Jack. Well, a few more than that. Probably about ten of them, if I really think."

His visitor's eyes had narrowed sharply.

"Oh, I'm expecting you to really think, Harry. I'm expecting that. Anyway, there's your start. Get hold of the ones you know. Each one of them will know some others who were there. It'll be like a snowball dance. In the end, we'll have everybody on the floor."

It sounded all right, but what about the time

element?

"I must admit, that does make sense," admitted Harry. "But you're not giving 'em much time, are you? I mean, tomorrow night is pushing it a bit, isn't it?"

"Yes, but there's no choice. Has to be done quick, while people remember. Don't forget, these young 'uns are out, every night of the week. Once three or four nights have gone by, they won't remember who was there. It has to be tomorrow. There's handbills being printed now. Should be here within the hour. Can you get a message out right away to get some of these kids in here?"

"I can try."

In fact, Harry had only been able to produce five young men for that first meeting. They were reluctant and suspicious, but Dandy Jack Westman could turn on the charm when it suited him, and he'd had plenty of experience in encouraging young newcomers in his boxing days. His enthusiasm, and the supply of free rums and vodkas soon converted the youngsters to his side.

"Tell you what's bothering me, Mr Westman."

One of them, a tow-headed youth in an immaculate grey pinstripe suit, raised a query.

"What's that, son?"

The young man tapped at the green printed handbill he was holding.

"You reckon there was about a hundred people here last night?"

"Hundred, hundred and twenty," agreed Jack. "What about it?"

The youth shrugged.

"Well, it seems to me you're gonna need the Wembley Stadium or somewhere. Not a bad group, Blast Off. You're letting the crowd in for nothing. That's a start. On top of that, you're going to let 'em

94

drink 'emselves stupid. All on the house. You'll need mounted coppers to control the crowds."

The other lads nodded.

"'E's right there, guv."

"You'll get half of London turning up."

"And the other half."

Jack was pleased.

"That's good thinking, that. Mr Edwards told me you were bright lads. Seems he was right. We're going to have to watch that. And you can help do it. Everybody who tries to get in has to have the O.K. from one of you."

The group looked at one another.

"Could try it, I suppose," said one. "Mind you, there's blokes about who don't like being told they can't come in. Could be some cross words, if you see what I mean."

Dandy Jack Westman's smile was very thin.

"Don't you worry about that, son. You won't be on your own at the doors. Be some friends of mine with you. What you might call specialists in cross words, if you follow me."

They followed him, grinning sheepishly. Soon after that, they had set out on their task of contacting as many as they could find from the previous night's festivities.

That had been several hours before, and now Parks and Yateley were walking into the lounge bar to check on progress to date.

They had scarcely passed from view when Jack entered the saloon bar. He nodded pleasantly all around, and went across to where Jan Stewart was waiting.

"Sorry love. Been here long?"

The strain on his face stifled what might have been a tart greeting.

"Only a few minutes. How is everything going?"

"Not too bad. Did you get it all done?"

Jan nodded, tapping at the green crocodile handbag.

"There are papers in here for you. I'll just hang on to them for now, shall I?"

His smile was swift and grateful. She knew he had no wish to read documents confirming that his father was officially dead. The reality was hard enough to bear.

"If you don't mind. Look, I've just got to have a chat with one or two people, then I'll take you home. Right?"

Jan was suspicious of his choice of words.

"Take me home?" she echoed. "You make it sound as though you won't be stopping."

His eyes were evasive.

"Well, can't be sure, really. Not positive, that is. A lot depends on what I find out in the next few minutes. I'll be as quick as ever I can, sweetheart."

He went over to the bar. Harry said.

"Your shadows are in the next door, talking to the lads."

"Good. Now then, who's here tonight that I didn't get to see this morning?"

"Quite a few. But I'll be honest, Jack. I think you're wasting your time with most of them. Old Tom Crabtree is here though, the one who found your dad outside. He was drinking with your father last night. Couldn't reach him this morning. He has this little job, four hours a day."

"Ah, I know him I think. Is he the one in the brown cap?"

"That's him. Don't come in a lot. Can't afford it, poor old sod. But he always sits with your father, when he does."

"Right, I'll have a word. What does he drink?"

The landlord hesitated.

"Er, no offence Jack, but I'd go a bit easy there. He's

96

very independent, old Tom. Won't mind having a drink with you, when he's ready. He wouldn't thank you for just taking one over."

Jack understood at once. Independence was one thing the older generation clung onto very hard in this neighbourhood.

"I'll just go and have a chat, then."

Tom Crabtree had been watching Jack since he arrived. The old man was conscious of the importance of his role in the matter of Albert Westman's death. Not only was he a long-standing friend of the dead man, but he had actually been with him on the night of the murder, right up until a few minutes before it happened. To top it all off, he had been the one to find poor old Pop outside, and to sound the alarm. The attention paid to him by the police and the newspaper reporters had made it quite clear that his position was one of some eminence, and Tom was secretly rather pleased to be the focus of so much attention. It was a terrible business, of course, terrible, and he was sad for his old friend. Still, it wasn't every day so many busy people made time to speak to him, or nudge each other as he passed them on the street.

And now here came young Jack, the dead man's son, himself a prominent man in some ways. Done alright for himself, had Jack.

"Evening Mr Crabtree. It's been a few years. Mind if I sit down?"

"Hallo Jack, I'm sorry about your dad. A shocking business. Shocking. I suppose you'd like to hear about it?"

Jack settled himself opposite the old man, nodding.

"If you don't mind."

Despite his anxiety to get things moving along, the new arrival was aware that he'd have to let his father's old mate progress at his own pace. There was a decorum

97

in these matters, a protocol as rigid as any to be found in more exalted circles, and if Jack attempted to hurry too much, he would arouse a good deal of indignation and resentment.

As his elderly companion launched himself into his narrative, Jack could see Jan Stewart showing signs of impatience. Good girl, that, and he was only sorry that she couldn't be kept out of all this. Still, she had done a lot of essential work that day, dealing with things that would otherwise have taken up his time.

"—well, I needn't tell you it was a shock. Couldn't believe it at first. Then I come back in here, and told Harry about it, and some others come out to give me a hand getting poor old Pop back inside."

Jack's face was concerned. Poor old bugger. It couldn't have been very nice for him.

"You did absolutely right, Mr Crabtree, and I'm very grateful to you."

"Only done what was right," intoned Tom. "He was a good mate of mine, you know. Thirty years. More."

"Yes, I know. I suppose you haven't got any ideas about it, have you?"

Old Crabtree was looking a bit mysterious now. This was something he'd been saving for the son.

"Matter of fact, there was one thing. I didn't mention it to the police, because Harry said you wanted things confidential. That was right, wasn't it?"

Ah. Jack's attention focussed sharply now.

"Right enough," he agreed. "What was it, Mr Crabtree?"

Tom coughed nervously.

"Well now, you won't misunderstand me? I mean, you won't think I'm being spiteful?"

Spiteful? What was he on about?

"No, no," Jack assured him. "Anything that might help. Anything at all."

Partly satisfied, Tom said.

"Well, there was this money business. Your father had a lot of money with him, and I reckon that's why he was attacked."

Oh, was that all? No secret about that. It was common knowledge that his father's wallet was missing.

"You could be right there," Jack agreed. "But that's not what you didn't mention, is it? I mean everybody knows the money was gone."

Tom tapped knowingly at the side of his nose.

"Ah. But they don't know he'd been flashing it about a bit. Why, only a few minutes before he went home, he got his wallet out when the boys' club man brought the box round. A fiver, he put in. From you and him, he said it was."

"That's right, yes, but that's usual."

"He doesn't usually wave his wallet about quite so much. I told him at the time, I said, you ought to keep that down a bit. He only laughed."

Keeping his voice low, Jack leaned over the table.

"But there was only the usual people in, surely? People you've known for years. According to Harry, anyway."

This was the piece of information Tom Crabtree had been saving. Nodding heavily, he too leaned forward.

"Drinking, yes. All regulars. Harry's quite right. But you can't expect him to notice every time somebody goes in the bog."

The old man paused for effect. Successfully. Jack wasn't going to hurry him now, of all times.

"There was a young feller come in, from the lounge bar, just when the box was going round. Only wanted the bog. Went straight in there, did whatever he had to do, then went back in the other bar."

Any impatience that might have been gathering in

Jack's mind now vanished. He felt a prickling sensation at the base of his scalp.

"A young feller?" he repeated. "Did you know him?"

Tom's headshake was decisive.

"No. Not from round here. Stranger."

"How old, would you say?"

"Twenty. Twenty one, two. Round there."

"What'd he look like? I mean was he tall, fat or what?"

Jack began to question his father's friend, trying to pin down any feature that would identify the stranger. By the end, he knew only a few things. The young man was smartly dressed, with fairly short hair. He did not wear glasses, and had no kind of face whiskers. He was neither very tall nor very short. Not too fat, not too thin. He was, in fact, best described in the way dreaded by every investigator. Medium. Still, it was a start. A good start. And it provided a possible link with the goings on in the lounge bar. Even if this young chap wasn't the one responsible, he could have mentioned what he's seen to some of his mates.

"D'you think you'd know him again, Mr Crabtree?"

Tom pursed his lips.

"Don't know, Jack, and that's honest. Maybe yes, maybe no. Only saw him for a couple of seconds."

Can't win 'em all. Never mind, it was a start.

"I'm very grateful to you, telling me this. Could be important. Very important, in fact. Excuse me now, it's going to be a busy night for me. Can I get you a drink? Turning cold outside. How would you fancy a nice drop of brandy?"

"Well, very nice of you, Jack. Ta."

About to leave the table, Jack suddenly remembered one final thing.

"By the way, what happened to the old man's hand?

Did he happen to tell you?"

When he'd attended at the mortuary to identify the body, Jack had noticed some broken skin and bruising on his father's right hand. As a former boxer, he automatically looked at everyone's hands.

Tom Crabtree was looking vague.

"His hand? There was nothing wrong with it, not when he was here. I'd have noticed. Sat next to him all night."

"Ah well, don't suppose it matters, I'll get you that brandy."

But it could have mattered. It could have mattered a great deal. Jack had seen enough hand damage of that kind to know that it might mean his father had taken a punch at his assailant. If he had, somebody might be walking about with a bruise.

Perhaps even some smartly dressed young man who had no glasses or moustache.

Better get next door and talk to those kids. He'd really got something to push on now.

TEN

The slam of the front door echoed up the stairs. Cyril Bowers jerked upright. It was dark in the room. Must have fallen asleep, he realised, reaching out for the light switch.

"I'm home. Anybody in?"

His father's voice reached him as he opened the bedroom door.

"I'm up here, dad. How was today?"

Bowers senior was hanging up his overcoat.

"Bout the usual. You made any tea?"

"No. I was just going to put the kettle on."

This brought a snort from downstairs.

"Overwork will be the death of you, Cyril, mark my words. All right, I'll do it."

Leaning on the baluster rail, the listening Cyril heard his father go into the kitchen. Good. He went back inside the bedroom. Better get those newspapers tidied up, and the whisky out of sight. It wasn't that people spied on him, he didn't think that. But they did go in and out of his room, and his mother especially had eyes like a hawk when it came to spotting anything unusual. As he straightened the room up, he kept reminding himself of the need to act normally. He must do nothing, say nothing, to draw any particular attention to himself. So far as last night's business was concerned, he was in the clear. Try as he might, he couldn't imagine one item which could connect him with that old man. No, he had nothing to fear. Cyril Bowers was going to be all right, so long as he kept his head. And one thing he mustn't do was to flash his money about. His original intention had been to stand Bas and one or two others to a Chinese meal, which was their custom when one of them made a few extra pounds. Not this time, he decided. Bas knew he was short of the readies, and there was no way he could account for a sudden improvement in that direction.

"Tea up."

Cyril took a last look around the bedroom. It would do. Then he went downstairs. His father had switched on the television, and was waiting for the early evening news. Right bore that was, the news. Why the old man bothered with it was a mystery. Load of old rubbish about Africa and the Far East, politicians, trade unions, traffic jams and city prices. None of it was anything to do with them, but the old man would sit and suck it all in, then yack on to his mother about how to put things right. It was Cyril's private opinion that the only part his father understood was the football results. Oh, and the weather forecast. If the bloke stuck a cloud over London, there was a fifty fifty chance it would rain. There always was, anyway, so it was a waste of bleeding time, really.

Cyril poured himself a cup of tea in the kitchen. Too strong, as usual. Always was when the old man made it. Then he walked into the lounge, where an animated cartoon was in progress. His father did not look up.

"Er, dad, before the news starts, could I ask you something?"

His father grunted, shifting in his chair. Everybody knew he didn't like to be disturbed until after the news.

"What?"

"I'm a bit short, and I'm supposed to go out tonight. Could you lend me a fiver till Friday?"

He had all the old man's attention now.

"Five?" he repeated, in disbelief. "Do you know what night this is? Wednesday, that's what. Where am I supposed to get five quid on a Wednesday night?"

Mean old sod.

"Yeah, well," mumbled Cyril, "could you do me four, then?"

"Two quid, and I'm making myself short," was the verdict. "And I want it back Friday, definite. Friday, before you go out boozing with your mates."

"Right then. Ta."

As he took the extended notes, Cyril was hugely pleased with himself. Touch of genius, this was. Not only was he not waving cash about, the day after the murder, he was actually borrowing it. Hardly the action of a bloke with a pocketful of stolen money, was it?

The sound of the front door announced that his sister was home. Cyril wondered whether she would have heard about the murder yet. It was in all the papers, after all. Come to that, was he supposed to have heard about it? Nothing would be more natural than for him to raise it, if he had. No. Better not. It would come up soon enough. One thing he must avoid doing, was to show any particular interest.

In the hall, Sandra was shrugging out of her imitation

fur jacket. She was feeling excited, and rather pleased with herself at that moment. In the latter part of the afternoon, she'd had the sort of treatment usually reserved for TV personalities. It had started when that Julie from the stockroom came back from her lunch break.

It was a quiet time at the checkouts, and Sandra had been helping out sticking price tags on some tinned fruit. Julie had approached her, looking quizzical.

"Didn't I hear you telling the others this morning you were at some gig last night?"

"Sright," she confirmed.

"What was the group called?"

Nosy bitch. Not as if this Julie was a mate or anything.

"They was called Blast Off. Why?"

Julie was certain now that she'd been right. But she wasn't going to reveal all her hand too quickly. At the moment, she was the one with the news. Once she parted with it, any limelight would transfer automatically to Sandra. There was no way she could prevent it, but it could be delayed.

"What was the name of the pub?" she pressed.

Sandra was becoming intrigued now. There was something in this.

"The Hope," she replied. "Well, Hope and Anchor, really. What you asking me all these questions for?"

Julie called over her shoulder.

"Listen girls, our Sandra's in the news."

A couple of the others stopped what they were doing and drifted across.

"News? What news? What's she done?" queried one.

"You mean, what's she done that's fit to print in the papers?" corrected another girl.

They all laughed. Sandra put down the little hand-machine she'd been using.

"All right Julie, you've had your little laugh. What's the big mystery?"

There was no point in further delay. Reluctantly, Julie handed over the spotlight.

"Nothing, really. Just some old geezer got himself murdered at your do last night. Wasn't you done him, was it?"

"Coo-er."

"Don't worry Sand, we won't give you away."

"Tried to get his leg over, did he?"

"Shut up a minute," protested Sandra, laughing. "What you going on about, Julie? Who told you all this?"

"Fact," reiterated Julie. "I was down the Wimpey, and one of the blokes in there had a paper. It's on the front page."

Realising now that there was more to this than some attempt to leg-pulling, Sandra held out her hand.

"Let's see."

"I haven't got it," denied Julie.

"Old Wilksie'll have one. Always buys the midday, for the racing," piped up an onlooker.

"He'll let you have a look, Sand."

"Yes, if you let him have a look, first," grinned another.

But Sandra could not bring herself to ask the supervisor for a favour. Not after the way he'd spoken to her the other day. Instead she would have to spend the rest of the afternoon in pointless speculation about the events of the previous evening.

Now she was home, and could get all the facts in the peace and quiet of her own house. The old man would have a paper, never failed. He was staring at the telly, same as usual. Her brother was standing near him, drinking a cup of tea. Perhaps they didn't know.

"Hallo," she greeted. "Seen the paper, Cyril?"

106

She knew something then, thought Cyril.

"Paper? No. Why, what's on?"

Without replying, she tapped her father on the shoulder.

"Mind if I see the paper, dad?"

"Eh? Oh. Here you are."

"Ta."

She took the crumpled sheets, and spread them out on the table. Cyril went over beside her.

"You won a competition, or something?"

His sister was busy smoothing out pages and putting them in their proper sequence. Now she folded them neatly at the centre crease, and the front page stared up at them. There it was all right, just as Julie had said. Cyril leaned over her, and they read it together.

"Looks like we missed all the excitement last night," Cyril said. Then, as an afterthought, "or perhaps you didn't miss it, Sand. You was there after me. See anything?"

"No," she denied, still reading. "It was all quiet when we left. Not even a punch-up. Whad d'you think we ought to do?"

Cyril looked puzzled.

"Do? What can we do? It's nothing to do with us."

She tapped at the newspaper.

"No, I know that. But it says here, the police are anxious to contact anyone who was at the pub last night."

"Yeah, but that doesn't mean us," he insisted. "What they want is people who might be able to tell them something. What good can we do? All we can say is we thought the group was good. Not much help to the law, is it?"

Half-convinced, Sandra nodded.

"I spose so," she agreed. "Still, it does say here, anybody who was there."

107

The mention of the police had penetrated through their father's absorption with the screen.

"Police? Did you say police? What have they got to do with us?"

Brother and sister looked at each other, and grinned. Any mention of the men in the blue uniforms introduced a state of near-panic where their parents were concerned. Cyril, in particular, welcomed the diversion.

"It's all right, big Daddy. Nothing serious."

"No," agreed Sandra. "But we'll have to go easy on the drug-smuggling for a bit."

"What's this? What? Listen, if you two are in any trouble with the police—" began the older Bowers.

Sandra waved the paper.

"We went to this gig last night," she explained. "Some old man got coshed on the head, and robbed. Nothing to do with us."

Their father was not satisfied.

"Don't like you going to those places," he grumbled. "There's always trouble. Fights, and the like."

"There wasn't no trouble, dad, honest. You coulda took the vicar," Cyril said patiently.

"Sounds like it. Bet the old man wouldn't agree. In hospital, is he?"

There was silence then, and the bantering was at an end. Mr Bowers' face changed.

"Let me have a look at that," he commanded. Then, as he read the report, his expression became stony. Reaching behind him, he switched off the television. "Glad you two think this is funny. Well?"

Cyril shifted his feet.

"Course it's not funny," he agreed. "Not really. But it's got nothing to do with us. Could've happened anywhere."

"That may be as it may," replied his father, heavily.

"But it happened where you two were. Not anywhere. Did you see anything, hear anything?"

Sandra shook her head.

"No, honest. It was nothing to do with our part of the pub at all. And there was hundreds of people there, dad. Don't go getting yourself worked up."

"Worked up?" scoffed her parent. "Bloke's only been murdered, that's all. Harmless old man too, by the sound of it."

Cyril's fingers strayed to the bruise at the side of his face. Not as bloody harmless as all that, he reflected.

"They've probably got the bloke who done it, by now," he suggested.

"Very likely," agreed Sandra, who privately thought nothing of the kind. The priority at the moment was not to let the old man get all excited. He might start imposing curfews and things. There was one certain way to distract his mind, and that was to get it switched over to the important area of the inner man.

"Now then," she said brightly. "What would we all like for tea?"

Inspector Miller re-read the printed handout for the fourth time. On the other side of his desk D.C. McCall waited impassively for his reaction.

"A free booze-up," intoned his superior. "This ought to bring 'em in, all right. How many of these things are there about?"

"They're everywhere, inspector. There's half a dozen youngsters from the Hope and Anchor spreading 'em far and wide."

Far and wide. Miller laid the offending sheet on his desk, and pondered.

"I had a chat with Westman only this morning. He didn't mention this to me. Must have had it organised at the time. I don't like it."

"Probably thought you'd try to stop him, inspector."

"H'm."

The inspector leaned back, frowning.

"Now then, what's he up to? Let's try to put ourselves in his shoes for a minute. Let's assume that he's thinking his father got done over by somebody from the lounge bar. Some young hooligan. What does he stand to gain by throwing this do tomorrow? Does he think, for instance, that this killer is going to turn up in a bloodstained suit, or something?"

McCall's grin was slight.

"Not very likely, sir."

"No, it isn't. Then again, we don't know for certain that only one man was involved. Could have been mob-handed, this assault."

"Yes sir. If it was, they didn't all hit the old man. Shouldn't be very long before one of them comes up, with his hand out for the reward."

The inspector's voice was grating.

"Comes up, you say? But not to us, eh? To Dandy Jack, that's where the informant will go, if there is one. Not much bleeding help to us, that."

"No, sir."

Miller bent his head, to read the notice again.

"If it was only one man, let's say, do you think he'll turn up at this do? Would you?"

The plain-clothes officer shook his head.

"No chance. I'd leave well alone. The man's probably feeling a bit sick with himself, killing the old chap for just a few quid. Bound to be in a state, I would guess. He'd smell this to be some kind of a trap, and keep well away."

His superior was nodding.

"Agreed. On the other hand, supposing you didn't do it? Supposing you were just a young fellow who happened to be at the pub last night, then you hear about this free invitation. What would you do then?"

McCall smiled.

"I'd be there like a shot. Free music, free booze, and on a Thursday night when I'd probably be skint anyway."

"Exactly. You'd be there like a shot, and so would most of them. I think that's the way Jack's mind is working. Not many people will turn down a free night out. Let's suppose most of them turn up. Not all, just most of them. At this moment, we all know there were over a hundred young people at last night's little soirée. It would take as many police officers a month of Sundays to track them all down. This little dodge of Jack's," he. pointed at the handbill, "will bring in say ninety per cent of them. And, with reasonable luck, the ones who are present will be able to say who's missing. Correct me if you think I'm going wrong."

But D.C. McCall didn't think he was wrong at all.

"See what you mean sir. If the ninety per cent can put the finger on the other ten, we've got a whole new ball-game. Perhaps only a dozen people to talk to."

"Say, twenty at the most. And twenty with names, McCall. That is the point. Names and descriptions. Doesn't half make a difference to this enquiry, wouldn't you say?"

"Absolutely, sir. Could be a big break."

"Could be, yes. But is it going to be? That's the point. Jack's not going to come running round here with this information. He's going to keep it to himself. The question is, how do we get in on the act? And it's no use thinking in terms of filling the place up with officers. All they'll get will be stony faces."

They seemed to be back at square one. McCall coughed.

"You don't suppose Special Division might give us a hand, sir?"

Miller had been thinking the same thing. The Special Division was a comparatively new branch of the force. It had been formed primarily to infiltrate the drug scene at the street level. The officers were all very young men, with long hair, unkempt beards and given to wearing sweat shirts and jeans. The intention was that they should merge into the general background, gathering information, and they had been highly successful.

If he could borrow two or three of those officers, to mingle with the rest of the crowd at the Hope and Anchor, it might be a very profitable thing to do.

"I was wondering about them," he nodded. "No harm in trying."

ELEVEN

Dave O'Connell sighed and looked around him. The Red Cockatoo was a dreary place at eight o'clock in the evening. Wouldn't warm up for a couple of hours yet.

His brother Des had been talking to a man at the bar. Now, he came across to the table, and slumped down beside him, holding out some kind of coloured notice.

"Our old mate is a busy little feller. Cop that."

Dave read it, without much interest.

"What's it all about?" he wondered.

Des shrugged.

"Search me. Perhaps Jack and his team will be splitting a few heads open, trying to find whoever done his old man."

Dave dropped the notice on the table.

"Wasting his time, if you ask me. What time is Maxie coming in?"

"He didn't say. Probably be knackered when he does turn up. He was going to see that Sylvia. You remember the state he was in last time she was finished with him."

Dave chuckled.

"Lucky sod. Bit quiet in here tonight, innit? Fancy a bit of a roam round later on?"

His brother knew what he meant. If there was no excitement on offer, the O'Connells liked to provide their own. Dave's apparently harmless suggestion of a 'roam round' really meant looking for some club or put where they could start a brawl. They were men of action, and inactivity always made them restless, and consequently dangerous.

"See how it goes," muttered Dave. "Hallo, here's Maxie now."

Max Bloom was paler than usual as he joined them at the table. The brothers exchanged knowing winks.

"Better sit down, Maxie boy," greeted Dave. "You look as if you had a hard day at the office."

"Yeah. Bad for you, all that grinding away," agreed Dave.

"Grinding away at something, anyway," Des chuckled.

Max smiled faintly.

"Tell you the truth, I come unstuck. I was just settling down to a nice cup of tea, with this certain party—"

"—cup of tea?" snorted Des. "I've heard it called some things, eh Dave?"

"You're right. Did you get a nice roll with it?"

Max listened good-humouredly. Then he said.

"All of a sudden, we hear this car turn in at the gate. It's only her husband, innit? Come home early. Next thing I know, I'm diving out this window. Had to hide in this shed till it got dark. Bloody freezing, it was."

There was no sympathy to be had from this particular

audience. The two men exploded with laughter.

"Somebody up there doesn't like you," reproved Dave.

"You're being paid back for eating that bacon sandwich last week."

The frustrated lover grinned.

"Ah well, it's an ill wind. I went down to the gym for a warm-up. There was this guy there, wanted a chat. We could be on to a little bit of business, if we like the sound of it."

The brothers were interested at once. Looking around, to be certain they weren't overheard, Dave said quietly.

"What kind of business?"

"Ready cash. Wages."

Dave pursed his lips, doubtfully.

"Wages? I dunno. What d'you reckon, Des?"

His scepticism was shared by his brother.

"I'm not so sure. You see, the wages dodge isn't what it was. We all know that. A few years ago, yes. All you needed was a stocking over your face, and a nice pickhandle. The mugs would take one look at you, and run a mile. If some brave bastard wanted to argue, you just tapped with your truncheon, and that was it. It's not like that any more. Not like that at all."

"Des is right. If the payroll is worth having, you need half a dozen of you to get it. Even then, it's shooters, everything. They've got dead crafty lately. Steel vans, dogs, bleeding hand-radios."

"Even then, if you do get stuck in, you might find you've got a dummy van on your hands. Look what happened to Ginger Baker's mob the other week, down Welbeck Street. Two of 'em nicked, and no cash."

Max had been expecting this reaction, and waited calmly until they had finished.

"You're right," he agreed. "Everything you say is

right, and you'll get no arguments from me."

"Well, then?" shrugged Dave.

"But this one is not like that. We're not talking about thirty or forty thousand quid, with half a dozen sharing. This is only a small job. All we have to do is walk in, pick up the cash, and walk out. No guards, nothing."

Des lit a cigarette, holding up a hand to restrain his brother from jumping in with some heated objection. Dave was a bit impetuous at times. A bit inclined to start shouting before he had all the facts. Des, on the other hand, knew that Max Bloom wouldn't be wasting their time. He had a head on him, that Max.

"You said it was small. How small?"

"About eight grand. Could be a bit more if they've been working overtime."

Dave snorted.

"I'm not sticking my neck out for that sort of money. Bleeding insult. If I'm risking five years hard, it's got to be for something worth doing. Surprised at you, Maxie."

Max was unperturbed at the outburst. He waited for the cool one.

"Hang on a bit, Dave. I'd like to hear a bit more. You say there's no guards?"

"Nobody."

Des pondered. Then he spoke slowly, almost as if to himself.

"If there's nobody there, then nobody gets hurt. Right?"

"Right."

"So we don't need shooters, don't even need clubs. Nothing."

This was precisely the kind of thinking Max had already been doing, before he had decided to mention the proposition to his associates.

"You're getting it, Des. All we do is walk in, like I

said before. There's no violence, no hard men to get past. So what's the charge? No robbery with violence, no armed robbery, what's the charge, eh?"

The business of reasoning was not Dave's strong suit but he could see his brother was paying attention, so he kept quiet for once.

Des chuckled.

"The charge is breaking and entering," he decided. "Burglary, theft, take your choice. I'm beginning to get interested."

It was too much for Dave.

"Well I'm not," he announced. "Buggered if I am. I'm not doing on five years for a couple of lousy grand."

Max kept quiet. The only man who could control Dave was his own brother.

"Now now Davie," soothed Des. "You're not listening, me boy. There's no five years at the end of this. We're tiddler-fishing. There's eighteen months at the outside."

"Only we don't get caught," added Max. "No way."

"This bloke, this finger, how much does he want?"

"He wants a thousand, no more. To him, that's a fortune."

Des made up his mind.

"Dave, get us another bottle over here. We'll have a nice drink while Maxie explains all this to us. No harm in listening, right?"

Dave was not convinced, but as always he was prepared to be guided by Des.

"Seems daft to me, but all right."

Des was satisfied.

"You've got the floor, Mr Bloom. Tell us all about this desperate adventure."

At nine o'clock that evening a large Rover swept to a halt outside a public house. Big Bill Yateley craned his head out of the window to read the sign.

"This is it, Jack. The Black Swan."

Beside him, Dandy Jack Westman nodded.

"Who's the guvnor? Do we know him?"

"Tommy's marked his card. He's all right."

They climbed out, pulling their jackets straight. This was the fifth pub they'd visited so far that evening, and there were several more on the list. Yateley had open the door for Jack to enter, then followed him in.

The bartender saw them arrive, and quietly went through a door behind him, to return with a large florid man in a chequered waistcoat.

Dandy Jack knew this must be the landlord.

"Mr Cooper? I'm Jack Westman."

"Pleased to meet you, Jack. Name is Andy. They told me you might look in. Sorry to hear your bad news. Gonna have one?"

They shook hands.

"Just a drop of lime juice in some soda water, if you don't mind. Got a big night on, lot of calls."

"I understand. Well, we've got your notices stuck up everywhere, as you can see. On top of that, we're spreading as much as we can by word of mouth."

Jack took the extended drink, and nodded.

"Cheers. Yes, I'm obliged to you."

"Not at all. Anything I can do, you know. Terrible business. Hope you get the bastard who done it."

The visitor smiled grimly.

"Well, by the look of things round here, it won't be your fault if I don't. I'll be giving a bit of a party when this is all over. Hope you and your mussus will be able to come. Be a nice do, I promise you."

"We shall look forward to it. Ta."

In the other bar, Bas and some other young people were discussing the leaflet announcing the free night out at the Hope and Anchor.

"What do you reckon, Bas? Think it's worth a look?" queried one.

Bas heaved his shoulders.

"What can we lose? Half a gallon of petrol is all it'll cost. Don't know about you, but if I'm going to be doing any drinking tomorrow night, somebody else is going to have to pay. Might as well be these people."

"That's right enough," agreed another. "I'm near boracic now. Might be a laugh anyway."

Another youth disagreed.

"I dunno. Bit creepy, it strikes me. After the murder, and all."

He was shouted down on all sides.

"What you worried about, ghosts?"

"Hold me hand, mother, he's rattling his chains."

"Look out, the door's opening. Perhaps that's him coming in."

All eyes focussed on the door.

"What a disappointment. It's only Cyril."

Cyril Bowers came into the bar, followed by Sandra. Bas turned towards the bartender.

"Rum and coke," he ordered. "What's yours, Sand?"

The drinks were soon before him, and he handed over a pound note. Then he stared at the two coins placed on the counter.

"Dear enough," he grumbled. "Bit cheaper where we're going tomorrow."

The barman leaned over.

"Matter of fact, he's round the balloon, talking to the guvnor."

"Who is?"

"The bloke who's chucking that do tomorrow. Name of Westman. Dandy Jack, they call him."

"Go on."

Bas relayed this information to the others. By craning

over the counter, it was possible to see into the other bar. They were all interested to see this Dandy Jack, who was known to be a figure in the West End.

"Used to be a fighter, they say."

"My old man said he was unlucky not to get the title."

"Looks handy enough, don't he?"

Sandra did not want to do anything so undignified as leaning over the bar, but curiosity finally got the better of her. H'm. Not bad at all. If you liked older men, that was. He must be thirty, at least, but very well preserved for his age. She'd have to admit that. There was something about his face, the eyes especially. Something familiar. Had she seen him before, perhaps? No, not very likely. Real West End sort, he was, the flash clothes, the big money. Still, he certainly seemed to remind her of somebody.

"Does he put you in mind of anybody, Cyril? Anybody we know?"

Cyril was the only one present who hadn't bothered to look at the visitor.

"Shouldn't think so," he replied.

"You haven't even looked," objected Sandra. "Stick your head over, and then tell me."

Cyril hesitated. He didn't want to see this Westman. Didn't want to see the face of the man whose father he had killed. He hadn't meant to, of course he hadn't, but that wasn't the point, was it? What was done was done.

Then he realised all the others were looking at him. It would strike them as odd if he didn't show normal curiosity. Stretching forward, he took a quick glance.

"You're dreaming, Sand. Never seen him before in me life."

Sandra grimaced. Well, it wasn't important, was it? Far more interesting at the moment was the way Bas was eyeing her.

120

"Thought you was going to meet the great lover tonight?"

She tossed her head.

"Free country, innit? Nobody tells me where to go."

The others were busy speculating about the following evening.

"I spose we're all going, aren't we? You'll be there, eh Cyril?"

Cyril bit his lip. The Hope and Anchor was the last place he wanted to visit. Tomorrow night, or any night.

"Dunno. I might have something on. I'll see."

This brought an unwelcome reaction.

"Something better than free booze all night? You might be joking, old Cyril."

"Well, like I say, it's nothing definite. I'll have to see."

One of the others nudged his companion.

"You're forgetting what a busy man our Cyril is. Specially Thursdays. It's a toss-up whether he's taking out Miss World, or starring on the telly."

"Oh, yes. What show was that again? Horse of the Year, wasn't it?"

"Don't you worry, when they start pouring out that free booze, he'll be the first one up at the bar."

Late that night, Cyril went home alone. Sandra had pushed off somewhere with Bas, and he wasn't sorry to be free of her. He needed to think. One quick glance had been enough for him to see Jack Westman the way he had appeared in that photograph from the old man's wallet. It didn't seem possible he could have turned up in this part of London, so far from the Hope and Anchor. Cyril had no way of knowing that the Black Swan was only one of thirty leading public houses on Jack Westman's list, or that Georgie Parks was visiting thirty others. To him, it was a direct line from his own local back to the scene of last night's terrible accident.

Because, of course, it had been an accident, hadn't it? Anybody half reasonable would know that, without being told. He was no murderer. Not him, not Cyril Bowers. Never. You could ask anybody. He wasn't the type. Get in a fight, yes, he'd do that. Might even do naughties, if he was upset. But murder? No way.

His mind turned this way and that, as he turned over in his head all the arguments that could be put forward in his favour. Besides, the old man probably had a very thin skull. You read that in the papers sometimes. Something to do with the bone. There were people, walking about, with skulls no thicker than a sheet of newspaper. You read about it all the time. Anything could kill them. Banging their head against a door, anything. That was probably what it was, he decided. In fact, that was undoubtedly what it was. Didn't seem right, really. You't think people would be forced to carry a notice. Other people had to. His own Auntie Ede carried a little medal to tell people she was diabetic, so that if she passed out somewhere, people would know what to do. You could hardly blame Cyril Bowers if some old fool with a paper-thin skull cracked his head when he hit the pavement.

Then he remembered Jack Westman's face. He didn't look like a man who'd want a reasonable discussion about the thickness of an old man's skull.

He looked like a man who wanted to find his father's murderer.

TWELVE

It looked at first as though the Thursday night idea was going to be a failure. There were less than twenty people in the lounge bar of the Hope and Anchor when Blast Off launched into their first number. Of the twenty, ten were working for Dandy Jack Westman, and two others were plain-clothes police officers, although there was nothing about their appearance to reveal the fact.

"Eight, I make it," muttered Big Bill Yateley. "A washout, that's what this is going to be. Eight, out of a bleeding hundred."

Georgie Parks hid his disappointment.

"Early yet," he asserted, "nobody ever turns up at the beginning of anything. There you are, look. More coming in."

Four young men appeared at the doorway, to be greeted by two others, similarly dressed, who were checking on their right to entry. When they were satisfied, they waved the newcomers in.

Behind the bar, Harry Edwards muttered to one of his staff.

"You'll be worked off your feet at this rate."

"Wait till about nine o'clock, Mr Edwards. Be like a madhouse."

Gradually, in twos and threes, the crowd began to assemble. They were reluctant, at first, to avail themselves of more than one free drink. It all seemed too good to be true. But the bartender had been right in his forecast. At nine o'clock there were seventy five people present, and the early inhibitions about the free refreshments had been overcome.

"Three vodkas, one rum and lime, one sctoch and American Dry, two lagers."

"Rum and coke, and one Guiness."

"Got any crisps behind there?"

Satisfied that things were beginning to move at last, the landlord had retreated to the comparative quiet of the saloon bar. It would have been a severe disappointment if Jack's idea had not worked, particularly after everybody had worked so hard the past two days.

"How's it going next door, Harry?"

Tom Crabtree leaned against the bar, resplendent in his best suit. Tom had an important role to play tonight. Young Jack Westman was relying on him to have a look at the crowd in the lounge bar later on. The idea was to see if he could spot the young fellow he'd described earlier, and Tom wasn't going to let Jack down.

"Building up, Tom. Building up nicely now. Seventy odd in there. You all right for a drink?"

Tom tapped at his glass, looking mysterious.

"I'll make this do for a bit. Got a spot of business on, later. Must keep me head clear."

Harry wondered what was so important that it was

keeping Tom away from the free drinks. That it was connected somehow with Dandy Jack he didn't doubt for a moment. There was also no doubt he was not going to ask any questions.

"Well, just shout when you're ready."

Jack had said he'd be coming in some time after ten o'clock. He had no wish to spend the entire evening in the saloon bar, listening to the noise from next door, and Harry couldn't blame him for that.

At that precise moment, Jack was comfortably settled in his own flat, enjoying the muted strains of Tales from the Vienna Woods. He had just finished an excellent dinner, and was relaxing before getting down to the serious business of the evening.

"More coffee?"

Jan touched him lightly on the arm. He turned towards her, smiling.

"Please. You're a wonder, Jan, d'you know that? Listen, I've paid twenty pounds a cover before now, for food not half as good."

He had a beautiful smile, she decided.

"Flattery will get you anything," she assured him solemnly.

Jack leered obscenely and rolled his eyes.

"Anything?" he echoed.

"Fie sir, you mock a poor maiden."

"I'll do more than that if I don't get some coffee soon."

What an extraordinary mixture of a man he was. Nothing could be more settled, even domestic, than the situation between them at that moment. And yet, in an hour or so, he would be gone. Out into that other world of his, where she had no place. In the ordinary way, Jan did not mind that too much. She had learned, early on in their relationship, that there were areas in Jack's life which were barred to her. Places where the 'No

125

Trespassing' signs were clearly marked. Gradually she had adjusted to the situation, and certainly Jack adhered to his side of their unspoken bargain. His life with her was a separate thing, and no one from that other life was allowed to intrude. But this matter of his father's murder was somehow different. He had been pre-occupied, irritable at times, and, most significant of all, unreliable about his timekeeping. Jack was always most scrupulous about that. If he said he'd be home at a certain time, then he would keep his word. But these last two days had been a jumble of sudden departures, spoiled meals, unkept appointments.

It was understandable that he would be deeply upset, because he had loved his father very much, but Jan knew there was more to it than that. If only he would let her help him with whatever it was, she sighed.

For his part, Jack was only half-listening to the music. He was watching the girl beside him, thinking about her. If he had ever done anything clever in his life, he decided, it had been the finding of Jan Stewart. She was right for him, in every possible way, and if only things had stayed the way they were—still. Those were the big words, weren't they? If only. How many people had come to some crossroad in their lives, agonising about 'if only'?

Might as well get it over with.

"Jan, I think you'd be better off out of it this weekend."

The change of pace caught her unawares.

"H'm?"

"I've got a lot to do. Lot of people to see. It won't be any fun for you, sitting around here. Why don't you go home, and see the old folks? It's about time you did, anyway."

That was true enough. It was high time that Jan gave them a little more of herself than the occasional phone call, the hurried snack lunch. For all that, it wasn't a sudden concern for her parents that had prompted Jack's suggestion. This expected flurry of activity was somehow connected with the week's events, although she couldn't for the life of her see how.

"Jack, I've always tried very hard to mind my own business about what you do when you're not with me."

"And?"

"And I'm worried. There are things going on, which are affecting you, affecting us. It's more than your poor father's death, I'm sure it is. And I feel so—so—excluded. That's it. Excluded. Just at this particular sad time, when I should be helping you—and Lord knows, I want to—you seem to have shut me off. I feel so useless, no good to you at all. It's not a good feeling, Jack, being on the outside. Not when you love somebody."

He looked at her fondly. What a girl. Woman, he corrected. If only she knew how much he wanted to confide in her, share his terrible secret. What a comfort it would be to pour out the whole thing. But that was a pipedream, and must remain so. There were plenty of people outside who suspected what might be in his mind. Let them. Suspicion never put anyone behind bars yet. The task he had set himself was one he could not discuss with a living soul, not even Jan. It was highly dangerous, and there were a hundred things that could go wrong, things that could put him in prison for life. It only needed one chink in his armour, for everything to go wrong. Besides which, he reminded himself, if there was any hint that Jan had any foreknowledge of his plan, that would make her an accessory. He couldn't do that to her, not to Jan. She meant too much to him.

When he replied, his tone was serious.

"Jan I want you to listen to what I'm going to say, and I want you to believe me. Nobody in this world has ever meant as much to me as you do. Nobody's ever been so close. I don't know how I ever used to manage without you, and I certainly wouldn't ever want to try. This last few days, you've been like the Rock of Gibraltar to me."

"But I haven't done anything," she protested.

His face was kind.

"Haven't done anything?" he repeated. "You've been here, love. I couldn't begin to tell you what it's meant to me, knowing that. Being able to come home, at all sorts of funny hours. Not to a lot of questions, or shouting, just to a smile and a welcome. You've kept me going, Jan."

She put a hand over his wrist, and squeezed.

"They why do you want to get rid of me?"

"You're wrong there. Couldn't be more wrong. Looking after my own interests, that's what I'm up to. The week-end is a write-off, so far as we're concerned. Gawd knows where I'll be, half the time. You'll be worrying yourself, not getting your sleep. Wouldn't do you any good at all. On the other hand, if you go and stay with your parents for a couple of days, you'll be glad to get back here, funny hours and all."

That was certainly true. Time spent at home was divided evenly between trying to stir her mother into revolt against her father's tyrannical domination, and keeping her temper when the male parent was present. His smug self-satisfaction was like a red rag to the free-ranging spirit known as Jan Stewart. Jack's assessment was shrewd, she admitted. A weekend at home would send her scurrying thankfully back to the flat.

"But there's the funeral," she began.

"No."

The rejection was flat and emphatic. Seeing the quick hurt in her eyes, Jack realised he had spoken too sharply.

"Sorry, I didn't mean to bark. But no, Jan. It really wouldn't be a good idea for you to come. There'll be the odd reporter there, maybe even a cameraman. You'd stick out like a sore thumb. We've been lucky with the papers, so far. They haven't cottoned on to you, or perhaps they just haven't bothered. But the funeral s Saturday morning, and the Sunday papers are twice the size of the dailies. They have to fill them up with something. They wouldn't miss a lovely-looking girl like you, a girl with obvious class, turning up at an East End funeral. I can just imagine it. 'Mystery beauty at last rites', or something."

"I wouldn't care—"

"—but I would," he interrupted her firmly. "I should care a lot. And after a while, so would you. Imagine the faces that would be pulled down in Bromley."

He was referring to her parents again. Not to mention all their dear friends and neighbours. Jan knew he was right.

"There'll be things to do afterwards," she argued, but it was a faint protest.

"Nothing I can't cope with. I'll take 'em back to the old man's place for a drink and a sandwich. The local women will do that for me. They'll want to, anyway. Everybody thought the world of the old man."

And so it was settled. They talked for a few more minutes, then Jack looked at his watch, and made a face.

"Time to go," he announced. The shindig down at the Hope and Anchor would be going at full blast by this time.

"Shall I wait up?"

He stroked the shining hair absently.

"I wouldn't. Get on the phone to your ma, and fix up about the weekend. When you've done that, you can

129

put some of your horrible music on for a bit. You always do anyway, the minute I shut the door."

They smiled affectionately at each other.

"I'll leave some coffee on a low heat," she murmured. "Oh, and if there's anything you want, when you come home, you'll wake me up, won't you?"

"What sort of anything?" he teased.

"Well, you might want to talk or something.

"Something?"

She stroked gently at his face.

"Oh yes, please. Especially something."

The atmosphere in the lounge bar of the Hope and Anchor was stifling. Early inhibitions about the evening had long been borne away, on a fast-flowing current of free drinks.

Bas sat at the bar, staring into the top of his glass, and musing. Funny lot, women. Take that Sandra, for instance. The previous evening she had been all over him, and now she was hardly speaking at all. True enough, she was with Donnie, but that didn't stop her from tipping him the odd wink now and then. It wasn't as though she was afraid of Donnie, or wanted to avoid a fight. Bas could settle him easily, great bag of lard, and she would know that. No, it was something else, he decided. Something he'd done, or she imagined he'd done. Chances were she would probably never tell him, either. Because they were like that, women were. You never knew what went on inside their heads. They were—er—there was a word for it. They were, hang on, it was coming.

"Unpredictable."

Without being conscious of it, Basil spoke the word aloud.

"You talking to me?"

Beside him, a young man turned and stared into his

face. Bas shook his head.

"No," he declared solemnly. "Thinking out loud. They're unpredictable, they are."

"Who are?"

"Women."

"Oh."

His neighbour lost interest at once, and turned away. A few tables away, the object of this exchange sat twiddling morosely with her cigarette. Sandra had already drunk more than her usual limit, and there was still an hour to go. Donnie was wishing they hadn't come. Drunks were always a bloody nuisance, and a drunken girl was the worst of the lot.

"Wish you'd cheer up a bit, Sand."

"I'm all right. Just leave me alone."

But Sandra was not all right. She hadn't been all right all that day, and the gin was doing nothing to improve her state of mind. On that Thursday morning she had woken up feeling very differently. Bas had been all she had hoped for the previous evening, and she had decided that Donnie must be ditched without delay. How this was to be done was something she could dwell on with pleasure throughout the rest of the day. Sandra was undecided yet as to whether she wanted the two young men to fight over her. On the one hand, it wouldn't really be fair, because she'd already made up her mind to switch her affections to Bas. On the other hand, the idea of the two of them slugging it out over her was not without appeal.

When the slamming of the front door announced Cyril's departure for work, she pushed back the covers and rolled out of bed. Standing before the mirror, she arched her body, turning this way and that to admire the various angles. Why shouldn't they fight over her? She was certainly worth having, no doubt about that. Especially her legs. They were her best feature. Long

131

and straight, and when she stood on tiptoe, like this, every line stood out. Then she ran an anxious finger along the side of her calves. H'm. Better be on the safe side. A couple of strokes with Cyril's shaver would take care of that.

She always felt like an intruder going into his room, which indeed she was. Although the house was empty, she still peered nervously around before opening his door and stepping inside. Blimey, what an untidy devil he was. Newspapers all over the bed. Wait a minute.

Bending over, she stared at the printed sheets. There were two different newspapers, both folded open to display the report of the murder at the Hope and Anchor. Well, so what? Naturally Cyril would be interested, just as she was. After all, they'd both been there. Yes, but hang on. When she'd come home from work the night before, Cyril had said he didn't know anything about it. Why should he say that, if he had two newspapers upstairs, full of the story?

Oh, do wake up, Sandra Bowers. Get the cotton wool out of your skull. Naturally, after you told Cyril the story, he bought a couple of papers, later that night, didn't he? Now then, where's that shaver? Perhaps he'd stuck it in the wardrobe again. She opened the door, and stared at the empty whisky bottle confronting her. That wasn't like Cyril, to have a bottle in his room. Besides, that was five quid's worth. Cyril hadn't got five quid to splash out like that. She'd seen her father lend him three pounds, only the night before. And all last evening he'd been moaning about how broke he was. Kept going on about it. Something funny going on here.

She sat down on the bed, thinking.

She and her brother had been together most of the evening, along with Bas and the rest. He hadn't bought any bottle of whisky, she was quite sure of that. Nor newspapers, neither. At the end of the night of course, she'd been alone with Bas. But the pub had been shut then. She'd seen Cyril set off for home. There was nowhere at that hour of the night for anyone to buy newspapers, and bottles of scotch. So? He'd already had them earlier in the day. No great mystery, there.

Perhaps not. But if it was no mystery, he must have had the papers before she got back from work. So why did he say he knew nothing about what had happened the night before? Because, you silly imitation Charlie's Angel, he hadn't got round to reading them, that was all. As soon as he heard the story, then he read them, of course he did. Yes, but wait a minute.

Cyril never bought an evening paper. Not even one. But yesterday he bought two. There could only have been one reason for that. There was something in them he wanted to read. Something important enough to justify buying them both.

And then there was the whisky.

She picked up one of the papers, and glanced at the story. Then her eyes fixed suddenly on a small inset photograph. A photograph of a young man in boxing gear. That was why she thought that man's face had been familiar, in the pub the night before. This was him, of course, the son of the dead man. Only it hadn't been the photograph in the newspaper that she had remembered. It had been the photograph she picked up from the floor in her brother's room, long before the paper had been printed.

Suddenly, she became afraid. Afraid of her own thoughts, of what she had discovered. Afraid of what was going to happen. It was unthinkable that Cyril could have killed that old man. No, it wasn't that. Cyril had his faults, true enough, but he wasn't like that. But he was mixed up in it, somehow, knew something. And there was only one person who had any influence over Cyril, only one who was always with him. Basil. He

133

could have done it. There was hardness in that Bas, and it would be well within his character to go bashing that poor old sod over the head. And to think that only last night she'd been alone with him. She'd let him—Sandra shivered.

"You all right, Sand?"

Donnie's voice cut into her reverie.

"Eh? Oh, yes. Yes, I'm all right."

"You're shivering," he accused. "Got a bit of a cold coming?"

"No. No, really."

"I'll get you a drop of something warm. Won't be a tick."

Before she could prevent him, Donnie had left her sitting alone. And at once, here was Bas, standing over her.

"You're quiet tonight."

"Am I?"

She couldn't bring herself to look at him. Bas was puzzled.

"Not worried about Donnie, are you? You needn't be. I'll fix him quick, if he starts anything."

He'd chosen the wrong words, unaware of the mental images of himself which had been chasing around in Sandra's mind for the past fourteen hours. She blurted out, without thinking.

"I'm sure you will. Like you did Tuesday."

Bas stared down at her, totally uncomprehending. He hadn't had any trouble with Donnie on Tuesday night. Hardly spoke to him.

Sandra was cursing inwardly. That has been a stupid thing to say. She hadn't meant to. It just sort of came out. She had to stop this, before it got out of control. Whatever Bas may have done, Cyril was mixed up in it somewhere. She had to think of her brother. It was suddenly essential not to draw any attention to Bas and

134

herself.

Standing up, she whispered fiercely in his ear.

"Look here, I know what I know, but you needn't worry yourself. I've got to keep my mouth shut, for Cyril's sake. But you just leave me alone, that's all. Lay a finger on me, and I'm straight to the law. I mean it."

What was she on about?

"Hello Bas, you want a drink?"

Donnie's cheerful voice interrupted them. Whatever was on Sandra's mind would have to wait.

"Er, no. Got one over there, ta."

He elbowed his way back to the bar, to find his glass had been removed. Well, so what? It was all down to Larkin.

"Let's have a scotch and American Dry, please."

The drink was quickly placed before hom.

"Your friend not coming tonight, then?"

The bartender's voice was casual.

"Friend? I've got lots of friends."

"Yes, but this particular one, I mean. Sat there with you on Tuesday night. Hardly left the bar."

"Oh, him? No, he's got something else on. Why, can I take his free booze home with me?"

That brought him a smile.

"I doubt it. This little lot's costing enough as it is."

The man behind the bar moved away, and began speaking to someone further along. Nosy sod. What had it got to do with him, whether Cyril was here or not? What with him and Sandra, with her 'she had to think of Cyril'. Bas was wishing his mate had turned up. Perhaps he could explain the mystery.

Unless—

No, that was ridiculous.

But the thought would not be dismissed. Suppose Cyril had clobbered that old man? It would explain a lot of things. Like Sandra's attitude, for a start. She would assume automatically they had been in it together. No, it was silly, thinking like that. Cyril would never have the bottle to do anything on his own. But he had gone missing, that night. Chasing some bird, so he said. That was how he got that bang on the chin, diving out of a window. So he said. Bas hadn't really swallowed that one. His private theory had been that the girl's husband clipped him one, and Cyril was ashamed to admit it. But what if there wasn't any husband? Or any girl either? That left the bruise on the jaw unexplained. Why hadn't Cyril come to the pub tonight, with everything on Freeman? He was always on about how broke he was.

Bas began to think very deeply.

"Having a good time, son?"

He looked up, to see two men standing beside him. They were ten years older than the rest of the crowd, and looked out of place. There was something about them which warned Bas to mind his manners.

"Yeah, it's all right," he shrugged.

One them nodded.

"We're friends of the organiser, you see. He wants to be sure everybody enjoys themselves. There's a mystery prize too, you know. Got your ticket yet?"

"Ticket? No. What ticket?"

"Here." The man held out a blue cloakroom ticket. "Everybody who was here on Tuesday is entitled to enter. It's all right, there's no charge."

Bas took the ticket and stared at it.

"Ta."

"Now then, we realise not everybody could come tonight. They're still entitled to go in the draw. Any of your crowd missing?"

"My mate couldn't come," he blurted out.

The man took a pencil from his pocket.

"No problem. We'll put his name down and enter his

136

number. He'll have the same chance as everybody else."

Seeing Basil's hesitation, the other man spoke swiftly.

"Have to know it's genuine, see? Otherwise, you could just put all the family down, and we wouldn't know."

That made sense.

"Yeah. Right. Cyril Bowers, that's his name. B-o-w-e-r-s."

THIRTEEN

Inspector Miller stared without favour at the two unkempt characters who lounged in chairs on the other side of his desk. Sergeants. Just think of it. Sergeants, at their age. It was all very well, having people like this, dressing up and mingling undercover with the local youngsters, but you'd think they would make some effort when they were actually on police premises. You'd think at least they'd comb their hair, or something. Still, he would have to admit, there was nothing wrong with the neat report which he had just finished reading.

The landlord, Harry Edwards, had estimated originally there had been about a hundred and fifty people present, on the night of Pop Westman's murder. That had been a rough guess only, and when a proper check had been made, it had emerged that the true number had been somewhere between one hundred and twenty and one hundred and thirty. A nice reduction in the odds. At the attempted repeat of the function the previous evening, one hundred and six of the original crowd had attended. So they were missing at least fourteen, and possibly as many as twenty four people.

He muttered to himself. One of the plain-clothes men spoke.

"What's that, inspector?"

Miller cleared his throat.

"I said I see you've managed to identify twelve of the people who were missing last night. Any word on them yet?"

"The names are being processed now. If C.R.O. comes up with anything on any of that lot, we'll start with them first."

"Yes. Anyway, it seems that our friend Jack Westman has cleared a lot of ground for us. At least we know where to look for most of our possible suspects now." He waved the report. "You're quite sure there was only one man there last night with a mark on his face? The lighting can't have been much to shout about."

The sergeant with the fair, straggly beard nodded.

"We managed to cover everybody. We spent half our lives under that kind of lighting. You learn how to look."

"H'm. And there was only this one chap, the one with the plaster on his face?"

"That's right. It was a boil, the tail-end of one. Nobody hit him."

The inspector wondered whether he was putting too much faith in old Westman's skinned knuckles. He could have stumbled against a wall and done it. Anything. But his cronies in the bar had all been adamant that his hands had been uninjured when he left the Hope and Anchor. It would have been in keeping with the old man's temperament to try slugging it out with his assailant. At least it was something positive to be looking out for, instead of pussyfooting around in the dark.

"Well, thank you for letting me see this," he acknowledged. "The super will want a chat with you later, of course. And good luck with these people who didn't turn up last night. How soon can you get a look at them?"

The fair one shrugged.

"Bound to take all day, at the minimum," he replied. "Look at those addresses. Scattered all over the compass. On top of that, they'll be at work, most of them. It isn't something we can get covered quickly, inspector."

"No, I appreciate that. I know you'll be as quick as you can. Was Jack on view last night? You haven't mentioned him."

This brought a shake of the head.

"Not for most of the evening, no. He turned up, just before the end. Had a look in the door, then he went into the saloon bar, talking to the locals. When the group finished playing, his two bosom pals went in there to report to him. They were all three sitting around a table talking, when we left."

"Oh, to be a dicky bird, eh?"

"Right."

After the plain-clothes men had left, Inspector Miller sat for a while in deep thought. They had done well, those two. To be able to obtain the names of a dozen missing people, and without revealing that they were police officers had required a great deal of skill and experience. After all, they had not the clear advantages Jack Westman had. Piece of bloody genius on his part, that had been. Mystery prize indeed. A couple of bottles of scotch, most likely. Ten lousy quid. That was all he had needed to dangle, and it would have been enough to persuade people to volunteer information about their missing friends. People who would have developed total amnesia if faced with a direct question from an honest police inquiry. No, the inspector had few doubts that the Westman approach would have produced results. The two sergeants had achieved a great deal in securing those dozen names, but it was a racing certainty that Jack's method would have produced more. Quite possibly the whole lot. Well, there was one consolation. If it was going to take all day for two experts to cover twelve people, it was going to take Westman much longer to trace a larger number. And there was nothing to say the guilty man would not be traced among the names the police had. All one could do was forge ahead, and hope for the best.

There was one factor which gave the official enquiry a slight edge, at least for the next twenty four hours. Old Pop Westman was to be buried the following day. Inspector Miller was well aware of the protocol in these matters among the people in his district. It would be considered a very serious lapse of taste on the part of the grieving son, if he was to be involved in anything other than the ritualistic formalities preceding such a grave occasion. The inspector's eyes twinkled for a moment, at the involuntary humour produced by his thoughts. A grave occasion indeed.

He would have been less amused, had he known that the list of people to be followed up by the police did not include the name of Cyril Bowers.

Desmond O'Connell ran a hand through his thick, wiry hair. It was four thirty in the afternoon, and high time their visitor arrived. If he was coming. That was the trouble with honest men, they were unreliable. Des had experienced it all before. Some straight geezer would come up with a scheme, and as soon as he got one or two people interested, people who really meant business, he would develop cold feet. It was one thing sitting around in a nice warm office, dreaming up ways and means of cheating your employers. To translate those comfortable imaginings into the harsh realities of the stockinged face, the iron bar, was a very different proposition. It was as though his brother had been reading his mind.

"They're late," grumbled Dave. "I reckon this geezer's got some chicken blood."

"We'll soon know," soothed Des. "One thing you can be sure of. If Maxie brings him here, it's on. Maxie wouldn't waste our time. Or his own, come to that."

"He'd better not," Dave muttered darkly.

Des ignored that. His brother was always issuing veiled threats on all sides, and some not so veiled. There was no serious thought in his head that Maxie Bloom would make any mistake. Just like one of their own, Maxie was. If he said it was O.K. to go, they would go, no doubt about it.

The door buzzer sounded. Des grinned.

"I'll get it."

Outside stood Max, and a smaller man who was a stranger.

"You're here, then. Better come in."

Maxie stood aside to usher the visitor ahead of him. The two brothers inspected the newcomer.

"This is Ernie Barnes," announced Max. "Man I was telling you about. Got a bit of a proposition for us."

Ernie looked at his hosts. He'd seen them before. In his part of the world, everybody knew the O'Connell brothers, at least by sight. They were hard and dangerous men, but Barnes had no fear of them. He was here on business, and it was sound business, as he would soon convince them. If there had been any doubt in his mind, he would have taken the way out opened to

142

him a few minutes earlier by Maxie Bloom.

"Now, I want you to listen very carefully, Ernie, because this is serious business we're on. These people I'm taking you to see, they're hard men. If the deal is on, it's on as far as they're concerned. And once you're in, you're in. There won't be any room for buggering about, once they've agreed. And one thing they won't have is people wasting their time. They get horrible nasty if people do that. You follow me?"

"I'm with you," nodded Barnes.

"Well I hope so. If you want to change your mind, want to drop this, now's the time. And no hard feelings. Once we bring them in, it's too late."

But Ernie had no intention of dropping it. He'd always thought this robbery was a soft touch, or he would never have mentioned it to Jack Westman in the first place. Given the choice, he would have preferred to be discussing the details with Jack and his crowd, but the O'Connell brothers were well thought of. This thing was going to work, he had no doubts.

"I understand what you're telling me, Max, but you don't have to worry. This is cast iron, this deal."

And now here he was.

"Come and sit down Ernie," greeted Des. "You want a drink?"

"No thanks. Bit early for me. I don't drink a lot, anyway. Might have a few when this is all over."

They sat round the table. Des waved a hand.

"Let's hear the story, then."

Ernie began to outline his plan, in calm, measured tones. He had rehearsed this meeting in his mind with great care. The proposition would, he knew, be assessed as much in terms of his delivery as in the content. His approach had to be confident, his knowledge sound. After all, you had to look at things from their point of view. He was asking them to risk their freedom, on the strength of his story. To them it was no light matter.

At first, Dave was inclined to interrupt, but Des waved him down. Ernie's unhurried, measured delivery began to impress them all. He had brought with him some paper and a pencil, and there were no further interruptions as he gradually sketched in the essential details. Finally, he rested the pencil before him, and waited for questions.

"I don't follow the bit about the electricity," blurted Dave. "Tell us that again."

He repeated what he had already said, amplifying where it seemed necessary. After that the questions came thick and fast. It was about twenty minutes later that Des leaned back, and looked at Max Bloom and his brother.

"Well, what do you reckon?"

"Worth a look," said Max.

Dave stared at Ernie.

"Eight grand, you said?"

Barnes shrugged.

"On a good week. It depends on how much overtime was done last week. But over seven, that's certain."

"All right then. Seven and a bit. How come you only want a thousand for your cut? Why should we get more than you? It don't seem natural to me, the finger man not wanting a full share. I don't like things that ain't natural."

Ernie was unflustered. He and Jack had discussed this, and he was ready with his story. The O'Connells had to be tempted into this enterprise with the maximum profit to themselves. It was a small enough job to begin with, and Jack had doubted whether they would stir themselves under two thousand apiece. That meant Ernie's share had to be cut, at least on the surface. It wouldn't do for these people to know that a

144

second thousand pounds was to be added to Barnes' share out of Jack's own pocket.

"I'm a learner," he replied. "You're the professionals. I know the ins and outs of it, but that's not the same as actually doing it. You've all done it before, you'll be telling me what to do. After the job is over, it might upset you to have to give me a full share. I wouldn't want to go upsetting gents of your class."

Des chuckled. Clever little sod, this Ernie. He liked him.

"Satisfied, Davie?"

Dave was already grinning. The appeal to his reputation as a hard man was always irresistible.

"He's got a head on him, this one. I say we go. The point is, when?"

All three of them looked at Barnes.

"Payday is Wednesday. It's unusual, but it's an old arrangement the company's had for years. That means the money is there overnight on the Tuesday. So, it's up to you which Tuesday."

Dave and Max kept silent. This was for Des to think about, he was the planner. Des considered for a moment, although his mind was already made up. Once a job was in prospect, there was no poing in hanging about. All things having been checked, the robbery would take place the following Tuesday. However, it wouldn't do to let the amateur know that. He might get excited, give himself away or something. What they would do would be to look the place over during the weekend. If they were satisfied about escape routes and so forth, there was nothing to delay for. Ernie Barnes needn't be told until the last minute.

"Well," he pronounced weightily, "we'll have to see. There's a lot to be looked into, even with a little job like this. We've got quite a lot on our hands at the moment, as it is. But it won't be too many weeks, Ernie, I can tell you that. We'll let you know."

The informant was disappointed.

"I thought you'd say we'll do it straight away."

Des shook his head.

"Mustn't rush into things. That's how people get themselves in trouble. They see a good tickle, they go rushing in. Don't wait to check things properly. Next thing they know, they're spooning up the porridge, telling everybody how unlucky they were. We don't work like that, Ernie. That's why our breakfast is bacon and eggs. Mustn't get impatient. The money is there every week. Meantime, you just keep this little lot to yourself. You understand what I'm saying?"

Ernie nodded. The threat was large.

"Don't worry about me. I've kept this to myself long enough already. A few more weeks won't hurt. How will I know?"

"You on the phone?"

"Yes. Max has got the number."

"Well, there you are then. No problem. Meantime, keep away from us. All of us. We don't want you getting a bad name."

Dandy Jack Westman stirred his coffee. There was silence at the table as he did it. Georgie Parks and Big Bill Yateley had made their reports, and now it was up to Jack.

"Nice," he decided. "Very nice indeed. I think what did it was that idea of yours, Bill. About the mystery prize. I wasn't too sure about that when you first put it up, but it worked. No doubt about it. The punters couldn't wait to get their mates down for a chance at the prize. It might have been a bit harder to get all this info but for that."

Big Bill Yateley tried not to look too pleased with himself. George grinned.

"Look at him, puffing himself up."

Jack pointed to the handwritten list in front of him.

"What we don't know, and what we can't ask the coppers, is how many of these names those two plain-clothes men managed to get hold of. Pity they were there at all."

Georgie nodded his agreement.

"It was a pity Jack, right enough. But there was no way we could refuse to cooperate. It was a straight request to help the law in a murder case. Not just any old case, but your own father."

"I know that," snapped Jack. "I'm just saying it's a pity. For all we know, every copper in London is out looking for all this mob. Well, it can't be helped. It just means we'll have to be as quick as we can. What we do is this. We split this lot up, by areas, so that we each have the least chasing about to do. That gives us eight each to find. We won't get it all done today. There'll be the odd one that's hard to get hold of."

"Tomorrow night's our best bet," chipped in Yateley. "Bound to be out on the rampage Saturday night. Might even find a few of 'em in the same place then."

"Right. Now, if any of us comes up with the right geezer, there's two things to remember. First, and I mean first, no rough stuff. No shouting and raving. Just satisfy yourself you've got it right, that's what matters. Second thing is to contact the rest of us. No point in us chasing our asses all over the smoke for nothing."

The two henchmen looked at each other. Parks cleared his throat.

"What happens then, Jack? I mean, suppose we do find the geezer, how are we going to—er—deal with things?"

Jack stared at each man in turn.

"Early days," he said levelly. "Mustn't go getting all

worked up, about something that might not happen. I'll worry about that when we get there. You follow my drift?"

"Sure, Jack."

"Right, yeah."

They understood the position, and Jack was satisfied.

"All right. We're all going to be busy, the next couple of days. I know we'll see each other at the funeral in the morning, but there won't be any chance to talk there. Too many noses about. Let's say that unless one of us comes up with the answer before then, we'll be here Sunday morning. Find out how we're doing. O.K.?"

Both men nodded.

"First job, then, is to sort out who does what." Jack picked up the list. "Where's Burnt Oak, for Gawd's sake?"

FOURTEEN

Sandra woke up and looked at the clock. Saturday morning already. Thoughts of the previous night flooded her head, and her toes wriggled with pleasure. Knew how to treat a woman, he did. Not like that stupid Donnie, all thumbs and rushing about. Bas knew better than that. He was lovely, Bas was.

And you, Sandra Barnes, are a stupid bitch.

Yes, it was true. No other word for her, really. A couple of newspapers on Cyril's bed, and a crafty bottle of scotch in his wardrobe, and her mind went rushing off. She practically had Cyril and Bas running the Mafia between them. Too much bleeding telly, that was her trouble. Silly cow. As though Bas could be mixed up in anything like that. He was gentle. She smiled at the ceiling. Well, mostly. As for Cyril, he never could do anything on his own. Never had the go for it. Funny,

Bowers? 149

how she'd convinced herself wrongly. Stayed out of Cyril's way all the day before. She hadn't been very pleased, even, when Bas had been waiting for her outside the supermarket after work.

"Fancy bumping into you then," he'd said.

"Yeah, fancy. You'd never think it, would you? I only leave here the same time every night of the week."

"Got time for a coffee, then?"

Sandra hesitated. He couldn't do her much harm out here in the daylight. Nor in some cafe. And she was concerned about her brother.

"I dunno, I should be getting home."

But it was no more than a correct, formal tactic. Soon they were seated in the new MacDonalds, and Bas was leaning towards her seriously. He had also been busy with his thoughts all day, and he needed Sandra to get his mind clear on some points of detail.

Somebody had murdered that old man outside the Hope and Anchor on Tuesday night: That was a point of fact. His son turned out to be a West End figure, and that too was a fact. Sandra seemed to have got it into her head that Cyril was somehow involved. From there it didn't take her long to conclude that he, Bas, would also be mixed up in it. That was understandable, because he and Cyril were mates. Besides, that Cyril wasn't much cop on his own. That made it understandable, but dangerous to himself. Not from any real trouble with the police. Whatever people said about the law, they weren't going to pin something on him, just because some chick had hysterics. It was not in that direction that the danger lay. It was from the son. People like that didn't waste any time with courtrooms, and fancy lawyers. One bit of suspicion, and they started lashing out. Bas knew he could never hope to handle that kind of trouble. He would be out of his class.

And there was one other thing. Something that Bas

had been pushing resolutely to the back of his mind. An unthinkable, not to be considered item, which nevertheless kept pushing its way just as resolutely forward again. It wasn't the sort of thing people like Bas ever thought about, and certainly not in respect of a mate like Cyril. You didn't do things like that. Not ever.

You never shopped a mate under any circumstances. Never. So Mister Bleeding Dandy Jack Westman could take his reward, and shove it where the monkey shoved his nuts. Even if it was a thousand quid.

Just think, a thousand quid.

"Sand, I think there's a couple of little points we've got to get straightened out."

Sergeant Rook did not like Sunday mornings. The cells were always full of the flotsam washed up on the Saturday evening pleasure tide. It was the task of the station sergeant to pick his way through the human wreckage, and despatch as much of it as possible back to the outside world, accompanied by stern reprimands and awful warnings about the future. By nine o'clock, he aimed to have accomplished his work, leaving only the hardcore residue of people whose transgressions were of a more serious nature.

Now, he stared despairingly at the grinning, anxious figure of an old customer, who stood, eagerly awaiting the expected telling-off, before rushing back outside to get into more trouble.

"Michael, this is the third time in a month. You're using my station as a bleeding guest house."

"No, no, your honour. 'Twasn't me at all. It was the nice constable, that new one, lovely feller. 'Twas him insisted I had to come down to your lovely station, sir."

Rook sighed.

"I thought you told me you were going back on the building?"

151

"That's right, sir. Yes. Oh, definitely. The building, that's me, sir."

"Well, you'd better stick to it this time. If you turn up in my nick again, Michael—are you listening to me—?"

"—oh definitely, sir. Yes. Very careful, sir."

"—I said, if you turn up in my nick again, I'll have you for sure. You'll probably get five years hard labour, do you hear me?"

"Oh, that's terrible. That's awful, that is. Five years, you say? That's a long time for a man to be parted from his loved ones. Don't you worry, my lord, you'll not be seeing me again. That's a fact. All I need is the one piece of good luck. Can I go now?"

The sergeant nodded.

"This time you can. But remember what I said."

"Oh, I will sir. Definitely, yes. A blessing on all here."

"Out, Michael, before I change my mind."

The wiry little man darted out, clutching his paper carrier-bag. At the doorway he came face to face with Inspector Miller, who was just arriving. Michael gasped, and fled.

"Morning, Rookie. Getting rid of the desperadoes?"

"Morning, Inspector. That's the last of 'em this morning." Rook had not seen his superior since Friday. "Er, how did it go yesterday?"

"If you've finished here for the moment, get one of the lads to bring a couple of teas down to my office. I'll tell you about it in there."

Soon they were seated in the inspector's room, stirring at scalding mugs.

"How was the funeral, guvnor?"

"Good turn out. Must have been getting on for fifty people there."

"He was well liked, the old man. Glad they saw him

off properly."

Miller sipped at his tea.

"There were a couple of reporters there, but I doubt if it was important enough to get into the nationals. Have you seen anything about it?"

"Haven't had a chance to look at the papers yet. I'll be surprised if there is anything. Usually, one of the lads will quickly spot anything which affects our manor. Did you speak to Jack, at all?"

"Not about business. Just condolences, you know. Anything new come in here about the case?"

"I've seen nothing."

The inspector sighed.

"Well, we knew there'd be a hell of a lot of enquiries to make. I just hope our two dropouts will come up with something. They're not here, I suppose?"

"Not so far. Still, with their job, they were probably out on the street till four o'clock this morning. I expect we'll hear from them later."

Miller made no reply. He was developing a feeling about this enquiry, a feeling that time was not on the side of the law. There was too little information coming in, and far too much of the presence of Dandy Jack Westman and his henchmen in every corner of the manor.

"You'd better say that again, Georgie."

Jack Westman rested his arms on the plastic table top, and stared at Georgie Parks. Beside him, Bill Yateley kept very still. There were no other customers in Sid's coffee bar.

Parks nodded, and repeated what he had just said.

"I said, I think there's a good chance I'm on to the bloke we want."

Jack breathed heavily outward.

"Who is he?"

"Name of Bowers. Cyril Bowers."

Cyril Bowers. Westman rolled the name around in his head. Savouring it.

"Go on, then."

Georgie counted off the facts on his fingers.

"This Bowers was at the Hope last Tuesday night. He didn't come to the party on Thursday."

"Perhaps he didn't know about it."

"He knew. Definitely. Made up some excuse to his mates."

"All right. What else?"

Parks moved another finger.

"On the Tuesday, Bowers went through into the saloon bar for a sprinkle. There's no doubt about that, because when he came back he told his special mate that he'd seen a bird he fancied in there. Went off on his own to see if he could have it away with her."

"How do you know he didn't?" challenged Jack.

"Because there wasn't any crumpet in the saloon that night. Nobody had mentioned any, before I heard about this Bowers. After I got the yarn, I went to several of the regulars and asked 'em outright. They were all quite certain. No dollies on the Tuesday night."

Another finger was pushed aside.

"Bowers has a bruise on his face. It wasn't there Tuesday, but it was on the Wednesday morning."

"Ah."

Despite himself, despite his resolve to keep calm, Jack Westman began to feel a rising excitement. This was beginning to fit together, no doubt about it. But he must not let himself be carried away, be persuaded too easily. It was all too important for that. Especially, although the man had no way of knowing, it was of vital importance to the stranger, this Cyril Bowers.

"Anybody can get a bruise on his face. Somebody could have hit him."

154

"That's not what he says. He says he banged his chin diving out of this bird's bedroom. This bird who doesn't exist."

Better and better. But by no means enough.

"Any more?"

Parks bobbed his serious face up and down.

"Bowers is mad on bikes. He's got one of his own, and he's been getting behind with his payments. He always on about it. I went round to the shop yesterday, where he bought the bike. Told 'em I was from a credit agency, just checking up on Bowers, because he was after an electric organ. They couldn't find his papers at first. Then they found out why. Bowers' papers had been sent to their head office as a cleared debt. He'd been in, and paid off the balance in cash. Fifty one pounds it was."

Fifty one pounds. The old man must have had at least that in his wallet, when he was attacked. Probably more.

"When was this? Which day?"

"Last Wednesday."

It had to be true, and Jack knew it. But something within him drove him to Bowers' defence, until there was no shadow of a doubt he was the right man.

"It all sounds good," he said carefully, "but I'll bet a good lawyer could find holes in it. You got anything else?"

"Yes. Bowers never buys an evening paper. He waits till his father brings one home. Last Wednesday he bought the News and the Standard as well. On top of that," Parks pressed on, before his inquisitor could argue, "there was a photograph of you in his bedroom."

"Me? Well, that's no surprise. Most of the papers had a little bit about me, because of the old days."

Parks shook his head.

"This wasn't a newspaper picture. It was a proper

photograph, shiny. Like the ones your father used to carry around with him."

Bill Yateley coughed. Jack looked at him sharply, to see if he was going to interrupt, but he need not have been concerned. Big Bill knew when it was time to be a fly on the wall.

"This is very nice work you've been doing here, Georgie. I think we're going to have to have a chat with this Bowers. Still, before we do that, there's one other thing. I'd like to let old Tom Crabtree have a look at him. See if he's satisfied Bowers was the one who came through the bar that night, while my old man was flashing his loot about."

But Parks had foreseen that.

"Last night," he intoned, "I took old Tom and one of the others for a little ride in the motor. We went to Bowers' local. They both picked him out. No hesitation. And no pushing from me, either. Straight away."

Jack Westman drummed his fingers on the table. He knew he was running out of valid objections.

"This is very nice, Georgie. Very nice indeed. Where'd you get it all?"

Parks shrugged.

"From his own mate. Bloke named Bas. Greedy little sod, him. He's after the grand. Nice sort of mate to have."

"You never know what a man will do, when you wave a few quid under his nose. Do you trust him?"

The headshake was decisive.

"No way. Never trust a grass, that's me. But I don't have to take his word, do I? Checked it all myself. It checks all right. You gonna pay him, Jack?"

The question seemed casual enough, but both his henchmen were clearly concerned about what their leader would do.

Jack Westman wagged his head slowly from side to

side.

"Am I going to pay? Yes. Am I going to pay him? No. If anything terrible should happen to this Bowers, and his mate Bas is waving a thousand nicker about, what is any self-respecting copper going to think? He's going to think there's a connection between the two things. And it won't take him long to decide the connection is me. No. I want you to go back to this Bas, Georgie. Go back and tell him we've looked into it, and he's got it round his neck. Give him twenty quid for trying. And," he held up a hand to ward off the coming objection "—if he wants to argue, tell him it's his duty to go to the police. Tell him that."

Parks and Yateley exchanged a glance.

"But supposing he does?" queried Big Bill, speaking for the first time.

Jack smiled.

"You're not thinking, William. He won't go near the law. Telling Georgie, on the quiet, that was one thing. And there was a big fat grand in it for him. If he goes to the police, what does he get? Nothing. Not a red cent. And everybody will know he grassed on a mate. Can you see him doing that? Can you see anybody doing that?"

The others relaxed. Jack, as always, was talking plain common sense.

"You've got a head on you, Jack," muttered Big Bill.

"And I'm keeping it there. Georgie, when you tell this Bas to go to the law, make sure some other people hear you. Might be glad of a few witnesses, one of these fine days."

"Got you," acknowledged Parks.

There was an unspoken question between them all, and Jack was well aware of it. Aware of it, and ready to answer it. Reaching inside his jacket, he pulled out two thick envelopes, and laid one on the table in front of each man.

"I've been carrying them around for the past three days. Jack Westman keeps his word. I knew I could count on both of you to sort this lot out. Five hundred apiece, with an extra hundred for the winner. That all right with you, Georgie? You, Bill?"

It was a neat solution, and both men knew it.

"Very fair, Jack," agreed Bill, looking at his partner.

Parks nodded.

"Ta, Jack. Very nice of you. Still, we haven't finished, have we? I mean, we'll have to give this Bowers a talking-to."

"No."

Jack's rebuttal was final. The others were mildly surprised. He looked at each in turn.

"This is private business, family business. Nothing to do with you, and I don't want you getting splashed. In fact, I think you ought to sort out a couple of nice birds, and get off out of it, tomorrow morning. Spain, or somewhere. But out of the country."

It was an order. They knew that Jack was only looking after their interests, in his own way. Big Bill Yateley stared thoughtfully at his envelope, then picked it up and tucked it out of sight.

"Could do with a bit of a break, meself. How long, Jack?"

"Long as you like. But make sure you're away till at least Friday."

Georgie Parks had one last try.

"Don't like you being on your own, Jack."

"Got one or two things to do," was the reply. "Better on my own, really."

Much better.

FIFTEEN

That Tuesday evening, the Hope and Anchor was doing a steady trade. No less a personage than Dandy Jack Westman had been present in the saloon bar since shortly after seven o'clock, and he was in an expansive frame of mind. Anyone who had known his father, however slightly, was pressed into drinking to his memory. Jack, being the man he was, could be relied on for a large scotch in every case. Naturally, the customers felt obliged to remain in the bar after accepting such hospitality. You couldn't just drink a man's booze, and then excuse yourself. That wouldn't show the proper respect, and so people who had intended to stay for a few minutes only found themselves part of a growing crowd by nine o'clock.

"I'll take a drop more brandy please, Harry. You know where my special bottle is."

Harry Edwards winked, and reached below the counter. Jack had handed him the 'special bottle' when he first arrived. The distillers behind the famous label would have been horrified at the contents of the bottle, now being tipped solemnly into Jack Westman's glass. The only connection between that liquid and the description on the label was that it was the same colour. Well, if Jack wanted to keep a clear head, that was his business.

"Harry."

Jack leaned forward to speak to him, keeping his voice low.

"I've got to slip out for a few minutes. I shan't be too long. Will you stand the customers another one on me, as they order? Just keep a note on the slate. I'll square up with you later on. Oh, and if anybody asks for me, just tell them I've popped up into the flat to make a couple of phone calls. All right?"

"Leave it to me, Jack. Why don't you come through, and go out the back way? Nobody'll know whether you're upstairs or not, then."

"Ta."

Harry raised the counter-flap, and Jack went past him, out into the rear of the premises, and through the self-locking street door. The street was empty as he climbed into his car, and drove expertly away. Five minutes later, he was sitting on a quiet side street, waiting. This was the crucial time. Everything he had planned so carefully was going to depend on the timing, and once the wheels were set in motion he was committed.

A man walked towards the car, and as he got closer Jack could make out the face of his old friend, Ernie Barnes.

"Get in, Ernie. Is it all set?"

Ernie sat down beside him, and nodded.

160

"I meet the others at half past nine. We go straight there. I've worked it out very carefully. From the time I nobble the substation, it should take us twenty minutes to do the whole job. Barring accidents, we ought to be home and dry by ten o'clock. No later."

Jack listened gravely.

"Did you get any arguments about the time? Especially from that Dave. He always argues."

Ernie chuckled.

"You warned me about that, so I was ready for him. Yes, he did say he wanted to make it later, but I had a lot of mumbo jumbo about the machinery in the substation changing over to automatic at ten o'clock. The way I told the tale, I wouldn't be able to cut the supply after then. Des told him to belt up. It was no use getting a bloke with inside knowledge if you didn't listen to what he said. No, you don't have to worry. We'll be going all right."

So it was set. Jack took a deep breath, and prepared himself. He didn't relish what he was going to do next, but a plan was a plan.

"There's a roll of plaster in that glove box. Get it ready will you?"

Ernie took out the adhesive tape and scratched at the end with his finger nails till it came clear. He didn't understand what Jack was up to at all. Setting out deliberately to leave evidence of his presence at a crime he did not commit was the most ridiculous thing Ernie had ever heard. But Jack was a man who knew what he wanted, and it wasn't for Ernie to argue.

Jack was pulling a thin black plastic glove over his left hand. It was one of a pair he had purchased that morning from an ironmongers where the owner knew him by sight. Jack had gone out of his way to ensure that his presence in the shop had been noted. The right hand glove was lying on the kitchen table back at the flat. He

161

was coming to the hard part now, and took a razor blade from his pocket.

"You needn't look if you don't want to."

But Ernie could not remove his gaze as Jack placed the corner of the blade carefully against the fleshy part of his lower left thumb, and pressed swiftly down and along.

"Christ, that hurts."

Blood welled over the outside of the glove. Jack peeled it swiftly clear, and Ernie clamped tape over the fast-flowing wound.

"Good. Where's your plastic bag?"

Ernie had it ready. Jack rolled up the glove, careful to retain the blood on the inside of the palm.

"There you are, my son. You know what to do with that. Exactly the way we arranged."

Barnes tucked the plastic bag into a side pocket.

"I don't like this at all," he muttered, "but I suppose you know what you're doing. You needn't worry, I'll do my end all right."

"I know you will, Ernie. And you're right. I know exactly what I'm doing. Here's the spanner. Use your handkerchief. We don't want your fingerprints on there, as well as mine, do we?"

"Gawd, no."

The spanner went carefully into an inside pocket.

"That's it, then. Just think, Ernie, one hour from now you'll be two thousand quid better off. Nice idea, isn't it?"

"I'll be glad when it's over. Well, I'd best be off."

Jack put a hand on his arm.

"One last thing. If there's any slip-ups, if that bleeding lunatic does his nut and hits somebody, you keep my stuff in your pockets. Don't get that wrong."

"There's nobody to hit," protested Ernie.

"You can never be sure. Somebody turns up

162

unexpectedly. Comes back to the firm because he forgot something. Anything can happen. I don't suppose it will, but just in case. I'm relying on you, Ernie."

Barnes was very serious.

"You can do that, Jack. You could always rely on me."

"Yeah. Well, here we go then. Good luck."

"And to you."

Ernie closed the door of the car behind him, and walked away.

It was on.

Ernie Barnes stepped from an unlighted shop doorway, and swiftly crossed the pavement as the powerful dark-coloured car slowed to a halt. The rear door was opened at once, and he slipped inside. The car moved away.

"Right on time, Ernie. That's good." Des O'Connell's voice was crisp and business-like beside him. "You been drinking?"

"Not one," denied the recruit. "Not a drop."

"Good."

"Ask him how he's feeling. How's your bottle, Ernie? Not going to faint on us, are you?"

There was no humour in Dave's voice. Only tension.

"I'll keep my end up."

It was true, reflected Ernie. The actual carrying out of the crime was something he'd been pushing to the back of his mind. He didn't want to think too much about it, because he suspected his own ability to carry it through. But now, rolling through the silent streets, he was amazed to find himself unworried. No fears, no inhibitions. Mainly, he felt a calm confidence in what lay ahead, and beneath that, an odd sense of elation. It was a new feeling to him, and quite different from ordinary excitement, a joyous anticipatory surging in the blood.

Max Bloom said nothing as he drove them expertly through the deserted evening. Some people claimed that he had a supply of ice-water which he injected into his veins before a job. Max was utterly reliable in these situations, and his secret lay in his total distrust. He had no faith in timetables, machines or people. Particularly people. He would carry out his allotted part like clockwork, but ever alert for mistakes, betrayal, failure. And then he would erupt into violent action to deal with the changed circumstances. But always with calm, always with the ability to revert on the instant to his previous efficiency.

"All right, Ernie, we're here. This is your part. You wanted five minutes, and that's how long we wait. Don't forget how much we're relying on you to get it right."

The threat in Des's voice was clear. Ernie opened the door.

"Five minutes," he confirmed.

The electricity substation was protected by a wooden fence. Ernie hitched himself up, and was gone from sight. Alone in the compound, he took a key from his pocket and fitted it swiftly into the single door, which opened without a sound. The pencil beam of his torch flicked over the silent machinery, and he grinned with satisfaction at his own expertise. Those people outside would be useless in here. They could spend hours looking at this lot, and wondering which part of it affected the Watling Brothers factory. Even if they finally came up with the right answer, it was a pound to a penny they would kill themselves as soon as they touched anything.

There was no such problem for him. Moving to a row of switches, he lifted one clear of the retaining clamp, and pushed it upwards. The circuit was broken, and all the expensive electrical gadgetry at his employers' premises was disconnected. It was incredible how simple the operation was, and how vulnerable the factory was, simply because the owners refused to invest in standby arrangements for their supply. Well, it was done. Now for his arrangement with Dandy Jack Westman.

Ernie carefully removed the bloody glove from its plastic bag, and looked around. Where could a man reasonably cut himself, if he was careless?

"He's a bloody long time."

Dave O'Connell's voice was restless. Des leaned forward and put a hand on his shoulder.

"Easy now, Davie. He hasn't been four minutes yet. We agreed five. And there he comes. He's early."

The wiry figure of Barnes appeared, walking quickly towards them.

"Everything all right, Ernie?"

"No trouble. Even the gates can be opened by hand now. All we do is drive in, park behind the warehouse I showed you on the plan. That way, the car can't be seen from the road. Then we just walk in, break open a few tin boxes, and help ourselves."

"All right, Max. Let's get on with it."

Max Bloom slipped the car smoothly into gear.

There was no turning back now.

"Cyril. Telephone."

The barman jerked a thumb over his shoulder. Cyril was surprised.

"For me? Who is it, Ted?"

Ted sighed.

"I don't ask people questions. It's a man's voice, that's all I know."

Mystified, Cyril went into the small alcove, and picked up the receiver.

"Hallo."

"Is that Cyril Bowers?"

The voice was new to him.

"Yes. Who's this?"

"I'm Bas's uncle. He's in hospital, he could be dying. Road accident. Calling your name, Cyril. Can you get down here? East London General."

Cyril was stunned. Bas dying? Must be some mistake.

"How did it happen? When was this?"

"Half an hour ago. Look, there's not much time. Are you coming or not?"

"Eh? Oh yes. Yes. Right away. Just a minute, what ward is it?"

"Just ask for Emergency."

Oh Gawd. That was bad, all right.

"I'm on me way."

It was very dark outside. Cyril half-ran into the car-park, and leaped onto his shining scooter. It coughed and refused to start. Furiously, he tried again. And again. What a bleeding time for the bike to start playing games.

"Bit of trouble?"

Cyril couldn't see the speaker very clearly, except that he seemed big.

"It's the starter," he complained. "Sodding thing. Picked a fine time. I'll have to call a taxi."

The other man had turned, as if to walk away. Now he paused.

"Oh? Something important is it?"

"Got to get to the hospital. It's an emergency."

"Oh dear. Which one?"

"East London General."

The stranger seemed to hesitate.

"Well, if it's an emergency. Tell you what, I'm going that way. Drop you off, if you like."

"Great. Cheers."

It was a nice motor. Expensive. No trouble with the starter on this beauty. They swung out into the road, and accelerated away.

"Family, is it? In the hospital?"

"No. Mate of mine. Road accident."

"Oh, dear."

The car turned into an unlit side road, and stopped beside a piece of waste ground. Cyril was puzzled.

"What are we stopping for?"

The driver climbed out, without replying. Then he walked around the front of the car, and wrenched open the passenger door.

"Out."

"Whaffor? What's this all about?"

A large hand clamped over his shoulder, and dragged him from the seat. Cyril stumbled on the rough ground, and was suddenly very afraid. This bloke must be one of those mad sex-killers or something. He'd have to make a bolt for it. He lunged forward, straight into the outstretched waiting foot, and sprawled headlong to the ground.

"Oh Christ," he sobbed, scrambling to his feet. "What do you want?"

"Robbery with violence," explained his tormentor.

"I don't get it. I've got nothing worth pinching."

"You've got it the wrong way round, Cyril. You're the one who's doing the robbery. I've got plenty of money with me. It's easy. All you do is beat me to death, and take it. Like last time. Like you did with that old man."

Cyril couldn't think clearly. Things were happening too quickly. Old man?

"Listen, I never killed him."

A fist rammed into his nose, and light exploded all round his head with the sudden pain. Blood ran into his mouth.

"Wasting time, Cyril. Get started. Oh, your hands are empty, aren't they? You need some kind of a cosh. There's an old brick, there. Use that."

His adversary stepped back, pointing to the ground. Cyril hesitated.

"Might as well," he was encouraged. "That old man was my father. So I'm a bit younger, you see? You'll need all the help you can get."

His father. Cyril knew quite suddenly that this was the end of the line. There was nothing to lie awake for any longer. No police. No trial. No appeal. It was all going to happen, right here. Now. This bastard was going to fix him. But it was true what he said about the brick. It could be reached.

Swooping quickly down, he got his fingers around the rough hardness. It felt good. Now we'd see.

"That's better," came that maddening voice. "You look like a proper coshman now. Come on."

Cyril rushed at him, aiming a savage blow at his head. The head seemed to melt away as his arm swept savagely down. Something which felt like an iron bar crashed into his kidneys. The pain was excruciating, and Cyril cried out in agony.

"You dropped your brick. Pick it up, and have another go. Not so easy this time, is it?"

The desperate hopelessness of the situation surrounded Cyril like a wall of misery. Perhaps he could reason with this maniac.

"Look. I never meant him no harm," he protested.

"Really? That's how he comes to be dead, is it?"

"It all went wrong. The old man went for me. That's the truth. He went for me. I never meant to—I mean, it was an accident."

Jack didn't doubt him. And he didn't doubt what would happen if this snivelling rat got into a courtroom. Put him in a decent suit, give him a short back and sides

168

and a good lawyer. His employer would speak up for him, the neighbours, everybody. They'd probably all prove he was a victim of society. He'd get sent down, all right. But in a couple of years he'd be walking the streets again. While his father lay in his grave. A picture of that pitiful, ruined head floated across his eyes. Jack said thickly.

"Better get your brick, Cyril. I'm going to finish you this time."

Cyril grabbed at his weapon, for the final drama.

SIXTEEN

Dandy Jack Westman sat in the saloon bar of the Hope
and Anchor, reading an evening newspaper. It had been
an eventful day in the world outside, with the result that
the two items with which he was particularly concerned
had been reduced to a couple of paragraphs apiece. But,
fortunately, the reporters were skilled men, and there
was all the information he needed in the abbreviated
stories.

The body of Cyril Bowers had been discovered at
nine forty five the previous evening, by police officers
investigating an anonymous telephone call. The caller
had reported seeing what looked like a desperate attack,
and the police were anxious for the unknown informant
to come forward. The dead man was known to have
been called away from a local public house at about nine
thirty that evening, and so they were able to fix the time

of death with some accuracy.

With some accuracy. Jack smiled to himself. That was precisely the position he had set out to create. He turned his attention to the other report.

The premises of Watling Brothers had been broken into the previous evening, and a sum in excess of eight thousand pounds stolen. There was no reference to the time it happened, but that did not worry the reader. The time was recorded automatically by the fault device in the substation, and that might not have been discovered by the time the reporter filed his story. Or, even if it had been, perhaps the police were keeping that piece of information up their sleeves. According to the paper, they expected to make an early arrest. Well, let them. They had all the evidence they needed. Ernie Barnes had seen to that, and Jack had heard his complete report earlier that day, when he exchanged Ernie's share of the proceeds for a similar amount in used currency. That was the final link for them both. It removed from Ernie the risk of being discovered with money which might be traced back to the robbery, and it transferred the same problem to Jack's doorstep, which was where he wanted it.

"Drinking on your own, Jack?"

He looked up, to see the unsmiling face of Inspector Touchy Miller towering above him.

"Oh hello, inspector."

"Mind if I sit down?"

"Help yourself."

Jack folded the newspaper, and pushed it to one side. This might be the conversation he was waiting for, and then again, it might not. There was no hurry, after all.

"How's it going then, inspector? You on to that bloke yet?"

Miller set down his glass. The drink might look like whisky to a casual observer, but it was in fact ginger ale.

The inspector was on duty.

"Our enquiries are coming along very nicely, thank you."

Very nicely indeed, he reflected. On the previous evening, a young man named Bowers had been murdered, not very far away. The investigation so far had produced one vital fact which had made Inspector Miller sit up. It seemed that the deceased had been one of those people present on the night of old Pop Westman's murder, and was among the few so far untraced from that evening. The fact of his death, and the oddly similar circumstances of it, seemed to point to some connection. It was always unwise, in police work, to leap for convenient solutions, but there was no doubt about one thing. Any possibility of a connection between the two murders would bear the most rigorous investigation. If there was such a link, it would have to mean that the original killer was becoming panicky. And once he did that, it was only a question of time. Time and patience. Touchy Miller was well satisfied with progress.

"But you haven't actually got him, then?" queried Jack.

"Early days, Jack. Early days. I was wondering whether your reward had produced anything?"

"Reward? What reward?"

Jack's expression was bland. Miller sighed.

"Come off it, Jack. Every schoolboy in London knows you put up a thousand quid for the murderer."

"Do they, then? They know more than me."

The inspector did not pursue it. Not then.

"Where's your two mates, then? Gone off and left you?"

Jack Westman felt an inner satisfaction. They were beginning to come to it.

"Few days off," he replied. "Out of the country

172

somewhere. Spain, I think. All right for some."

"I agree. When was this, today some time?"

The man opposite looked puzzled.

"No. Couple of days ago. Monday, I think. Why, what does it matter?"

The inspector shook his head. It didn't matter at all. There would be plane tickets, passports, all easy to check.

"It doesn't," he denied. "Just not like them to leave you like that."

Westman shrugged.

"They needed a break. I'd have gone myself, but there's too much going on. You know."

"Yes, I know. Hallo, hurt your hand, have you?"

Jack closed his hand quickly over the revealing Elastoplast.

"Nothing, really. Screwdriver slipped. Cut my thumb."

Inspector Miller tutted his disapproval.

"Should have had your gloves on, Jack. Should always wear gloves when you're doing dangerous work."

"Gloves?"

Jack's laugh was nervous.

Miller leaned forward on his elbows.

"I've got a glove might fit you, Jack. There's a cut in it. Funny enough, the cut is just about where your cut is."

A worried look appeared on the face opposite.

"I don't get it."

"You will, Jack, you will. I went round to your place, an hour ago. For a chat, you know. You weren't there."

"So? I was probably on my way down here. You must have just missed me."

"Yes. Well, never mind. There were a couple of things we didn't miss."

173

Miller left the conversation hanging in the air. Jack Westman ran agitated fingers through his hair.

"Things?" he echoed. "What things? And did you say 'we'?"

"Yes. My sergeant was with me. What we found was a glove. Plastic glove, for the right hand. And guess what else we found?"

His victim was now clearly worried.

"Found? You've been in my flat? You've got no right to do that," he protested. "You have to have a warrant to do that."

"Yes, you're right. But I had one, you see. And you didn't ask me what it was we found."

"Go on then, if you want to play bleeding games."

"Money, Jack. A lot of money. A thousand quid at least. Maybe more."

"So what? No law against that, is there? Not yet, anyway."

Miller's tone was very calm, reasoning.

"No, no, of course not. But these were all new notes, you see. All numbered in series. Very tidy."

"So?"

"The numbers were among those missing from a certain burglary last night. Funny coincidence, isn't it?"

Westman stared at the table, his face set.

"Tell you something else, Jack. That glove we found was all by itself. The other one turned up at the burglary. There's blood on it, Jack. How d'you suppose that happened?"

"You're doing all the talking," snapped Westman.

"I do go on a bit, sometimes," soothed the inspector. "Nearly finished. At that burglary we were talking about, somebody dropped a spanner. It's got your fingerprints on it. Now, you must admit, that is strange."

"I'm not going to admit anything at all," muttered Jack.

Miller decided to end it.

"You're in it, Jack. Right up to here. Never thought I'd see the day when you'd try something as daft as this. The great Dandy Jack Westman. It can only be because you're so upset. Wouldn't have happened otherwise, I'm sure."

"Don't know what you're talking about."

"Then I'll explain it to you. Watling Brothers was broken into last night, all the wages nicked. New notes, mostly. A thousand pounds of that same money turns up in your flat. One of the villains cut himself, threw a glove away. There's blood on it. You've cut yourself, Jack. Won't take the doctors long to match the blood. There was a spanner dropped at the scene of the crime. Your fingerprints are on it. Jack, look at it from my point of view. Where were you at a quarter to ten last night? Because, unless you were having dinner at Buckingham Palace, you are right in the claggy."

"Frame-up," said Jack, hoarsely. "Planted evidence."

"Tut tut Jack, you know me better than that. You're as guilty as sin. You're going down, my son. Three years, I reckon."

Westman stared at him with hatred.

"You got a warrant?" he demanded.

"It's in my pocket. Now, you're not going to do something silly, are you? There's two officers outside. We'll just go out nice and quietly. No need to upset all the customers."

Jack stood up, breathing heavily.

"Thank Gawd you won't be on the jury, that's all. At least I'll get a fair trial."

"Course you will, Jack. You're entitled to it. And after the trial, you'll go away. Don't be in any doubt

175

about it. I've seldom seen such a watertight case, in my life."

I hope you're right, inspector, thought Jack. Brother, how I hope that. Out loud he said.

"Come on, then. We'll see if you still feel so pleased with yourself when a decent lawyer gets to work."

Inspector Miller chuckled. He was a happy man, at that moment.

"I've got you Jack. Really got you buttoned up."

They walked slowly towards the door. Harry Edwards called out

"You off then, Jack?"

"Yes. Bit of business. Good night, Harry."

"Goodnight, Jack."

Harry walked across to tidy up the table. Jack had left his paper behind. Back at the bar, he opened it up, scanning quickly at the pages. Same old rubbish. Nothing in there.

Harry thew the newspaper into the waste bin.